Women Warriors
Beyond The Yellow Gate

By: Cathy Henn

Women Warriors Beyond The Yellow Gate

Available for purchase at:
www.amazon.com

ISBN: 978-1723905452

Cover photo courtesy of Dusty Hardman

How to contact the author:

Cathy Henn

henncathy@gmail.com

Dedication

Going Beyond The Yellow Gate represents attempting an enormous challenge. My granddaughter faced such a challenge during the first year of her life. Born with multiple heart defects (Congenital Heart Disease or CHD), she spent months in the hospital undergoing extensive repairs. She took all the difficulties in stride and bore the pain, and she is doing very well now. She is my inspiration.

Acknowledgements

Thank you to my beloved husband, Karl (RawDog), for your love and support. Once again, you wrote all the best lines.

Thanks to Dusty Hardman for believing in me.

I am indebted to a special group of big-hearted people. Thank you scRitch, Ed, Gail, Alondra, Keith, Michelle, Margaret, Nancy, Paul, Ken, Hiram, Dan, laz, and Stu.

A special thanks to Bubba and Bud for coming over from *The Virgin and The Veteran* to help out, and thanks to Sassy's great-granddaughter, Sassy IV, for joining in the fun.

This book is a work of fiction. Quotes and people's names are used with permission.

ATTEMPT TWO

Chapter 1: One Mistake Leads to Another

Sunday's weather had been a triple threat, with the cold, the wind, and the residual rain from the day before. She had spent the day racing through creeks and drainage water up to her ankles. Finally, the clouds were retreating as afternoon crept on. Sunlight was drifting through the upper trees, and birds were calling to their prospective mates. Early spring in the mountains was a joyful time for the creatures of the air. Love was all around her, but all she felt was dead tired.

Finishing the world's hardest race was in her grasp if she could only keep moving. She had almost completed four 20+ mile loops out of the required five around the state park. Unfortunately, the hardest climb was before her, Jaquemate, the crusher of many a runner's dreams. She wished she would never have to face it again, but she had two more times to scale it in this race.

She started up the steep slope from the creek determinedly enough, but struggled through the mud and forest debris that had washed down in the heavy rains the day before. She was exhausted after nearly eighty miles of pushing herself through rough back country. The soil was inundated with water after all the rain, and the temperature was still chilly as the sky cleared. Fog was forming in the valleys and rising slowly up the mountainside; it was an ever moving wall that limited her visibility. She was tired, cold, and couldn't see, and she was frustrated with her progress that day.

There were all kinds of logical excuses for the mistake she was making, but it was still a mistake. She acquiesced to the mountain and moved over to the left to try to find an easier way. She figured once she achieved better footing, she would adjust back to the line she had been on. She checked her compass bearing periodically to try to stay near the line.

She was moving up more smoothly, but then she came upon a steep cliff band. Should she move back to the right, or stubbornly continue up? She hated the thought of retreating any further.

There was a long crack in the rock that she thought she could use to pull herself up the twenty feet or so to the top, so she stuck her fingers in the crack and started up. Her running shoes were wet and muddy from crossing creeks and from the day's rain, so there wasn't much friction, and they slid around on the rubbery flippers of lichens living on the gray wall. She stuck her toes in the crack and used her upper body strength to haul herself up. All those hours of training with weights were paying off.

Her hair had come loose from under her buff, a stretchy scarf that she was using as a headband, and had fallen into her eyes. She shook her head, annoyed, to flip the strands of hair away. She put her right hand up to grab what looked like a knotty place on a ledge, and almost put her hand down right onto the top of a snake coiled on the ledge. She heard its loud hissing as her hand came down.

"Oh my God!" she cried out.

She couldn't see it well, but it kept hissing at her menacingly. What kind of snake was it? Was it a rattlesnake? Was it preparing to strike?

Her fear of snakes overwhelmed her fear of heights; she screamed, and her hand pulled back reflexively. She let go of the rock with her other hand and then her feet pushed her body off the rock, as she was desperate to get away from the snake. She plummeted backwards off the rock, free *falling into empty space.*

It was all so fast, but seemed so slow. She would remember it later like watching a movie in slow motion.

ATTEMPT ONE

Chapter 2: Women Are Too Soft

When Amanda's husband explained the details to her about the world's hardest 100 mile trail race, she couldn't believe how difficult it sounded. She had heard about it before, but never gave it much thought. The race had five dubiously measured twenty-mile loops through the backwoods of East Tennessee. Most of the course was run off-trail through steep terrain and briers, with a horrific amount of elevation gain. There were no aid stations and only two unmanned water drops, plus your own aid from your car as you passed through the campground at the end of every loop. There were only fifteen male finishers and no women finishers, in over thirty years of existence.

She quizzed him about why there were no women finishers while they were out doing their evening run in the foothills outside of Denver.

"I don't know. Many women have tried. Apparently, the race director has thrown down the gauntlet for women runners," he said. "He says the race is too hard for women, and women are too soft."

Amanda's mind was blown away. "Women are too

soft? The race is too hard?" She increased her speed at the idea that someone might think that something was too hard for her. Her dark, curly hair was escaping from under her cap into her eyes, so she pushed the locks of hair up under the brim.

"Hey, wait up," her husband sputtered as she sprinted ahead of him. He watched her bare legs flash in the soft evening light. She was short of stature, with a boyish figure with narrow hips.

"So, has this race director ever done the course himself?" she fumed as Robbie caught up to her.

"Well, someone told me that he hiked a loop at the very beginning, back in the 80's when the race was easier, and he has done every section of it on book set-outs," replied her husband. His forehead was wet with sweat that was about to drip from his eyebrow prominence into his eyes, and he wiped it up into his thick, dark hair with one long, continuous swipe of his forearm and the back of his hand.

"What are 'book set-outs'?" she asked, suddenly curious to know everything there was to know.

"Race Management sets out paperback books at unmanned checkpoints all over the course. Competitors have to rip a page with a number corresponding to their bib number out of a book to show that they have made it that far," he patiently explained. "They have to navigate with their map and compass to find the books."

"Why was the race easier at the beginning?" she asked, sprinting ahead again.

"Amanda! I've been working for seven straight days in the ER! Slow down a bit!"

Robbie was an emergency room nurse, and he was worn out from a busy week, but still determined to get his run in with Amanda.

She slowed down a tiny bit for him, and he explained, "Whenever a racer is able to complete all five loops, laz, the race director, and RawDog, the co-director, add new places and more elevation, but the mileage stays the same for each loop, 20 miles, which is totally impossible, of course," said Robbie, who was working hard and simultaneously breathing and talking as they climbed a steep hill. "I mean, impossible that the mileage stays the same, but the distance gets longer," he struggled to explain.

They had reached the crest of the hill, and Robbie stopped for a minute to breathe in the lovely view of Denver in the waning sunlight, but Amanda urged him on. "We need to beat our three hours from last week. Come on!"

As they trotted down the other side, she asked, "So, this race director, laz, and his sidekick, RawDog— what a weird name—conduct this sadistic experiment every year to see how many people they can humiliate with this sick race?"

Robbie squinted and shrugged his shoulders. "*Mmmmmmmm*, well, sort of, but it really is a test of man versus the elements, a psychological and mental test of man's ability to endure against all odds..." He was responding to her sarcastic question thoughtfully, when she started screaming.

"MAN versus the elements??? MAN's ability to endure? Robbie! You're a chauvinistic pig, exactly like those race directors!" Her yell split the quiet night in two. "What about women? What about ME? Do you think I can't do it?" She was sprinting downhill now on the rocky jeep road, and he could barely keep up.

Robbie grimaced, knowing he had hit a nerve, and knowing for sure that he would be sleeping on the couch tonight. He stopped at the bottom of the hill to rest for a second, and she stomped back to him, an angry look on her pretty face.

"I didn't mean it like that, sweetie...it was only an expression. I should have said *people's* ability to endure, or *runners* against the elements," he said, quickly trying to change the course of his evening.

But it was too late. Amanda was livid. "You don't think I could do that race?" She had her hands on her hips now, and she was ready to fight. "After all the hundred-milers I've won in the women's division, and beaten tons of men? And after all the training I do, and the three sponsorships I've killed myself to get? And what about the fifty hours a week I work on my feet in the lab?"

Amanda worked as a researcher in a biomedical research lab, in addition to all her ultrarunning and marketing for her sponsors. She was in constant motion and had boundless energy, and Robbie didn't know how she did it. He could barely keep up with her on their training runs, and never beat her in races.

"No, honey, I didn't mean that at all. Of course I think you could do it, with the right training, with the right strategy, and with an injury-free season or two," he said. Robbie tried his best to placate her hot-wired head, knowing full well that her internal fire was well lit for this race now, and it was all his fault. He reached out to stroke her cheek, but she slapped his hand away, and turned and silently sprinted for home.

When they finally returned home, after nearly twice the distance and speed that they had planned on, Amanda tore around their apartment, full of pent-up steam over the idea that a woman could not finish that silly race.

"No woman can do it, *huh*? The race is too hard, and women are too soft? Yeah, right. I'll show him. I'll show all of them!" She was swearing under her breath as she clattered the clean silverware out of the dishwasher into the drawer, angrily plunked the dirty dishes into the dishwasher, and then viciously stuffed the pile of dirty laundry into the washing machine.

Robbie sat down on the couch to untie his shoes, and began to breathe easier. Maybe she would calm down in a few minutes, he hoped. He pulled a cold beer out of the fridge, avoiding Amanda in the process, and flipped on the TV as he sat down with his bare feet up on the coffee table.

It became ominously quiet in the kitchen, and suddenly Amanda was in front of him. She flopped down on the couch next to him, sat back and leaned her head on his shoulder and cuddled her body in next to his.

"I'm sorry I got so mad," she said, looking up at him with her dark, intense eyes.

He looked down at her, sighed, flipped off the TV, and relaxed a bit. It was time to make up. He held her shoulder with his right hand, reached around with his left hand and pushed her dark curls off her forehead, then strolled his left hand down her cheek, and then down her shoulder. Then he kissed her, and her body melded into his.

"Too soft for you?" she murmured, caressing his back.

"Noooooo," he breathed. "Just right."

ATTEMPT TWO

Chapter 3: An Unlucky Break

When she hit the slope below, her right leg was folded up behind her and hit first. She felt something give way inside of her ankle, and heard a cracking noise. The pain boomeranged off and away, then came back repetitively as she bounced down the slope. She tried to grab and claw onto something to stop her fall, but had no luck. Finally, she came to a stop in a little ravine, and lay there on her side, panting.

Her hip hurt, her back ached, and her forehead stung, but her right leg was throbbing in waves of pain. She tried to sit up, but fell back in agony. She put her hands up to her forehead and felt the wetness of blood seeping out of a cut, so she pulled her buff down lower on her forehead and folded it up several times to make a pad to stanch the blood flow. She gingerly palpated her hip and back and thought they were bruised and not broken. The ankle region of her leg had taken the brunt of the fall.

Lying on her left side, she was able to pull her knees up to her belly and take a look at her right ankle. No bone was sticking out, thank goodness.

She lowered her leg to the ground, ever so gently, thinking that it must be broken.

She lay there in that childlike position for a while, stunned, and not knowing what to do. Finally, she decided to try to stand up. She thought she could use her hiking poles to help with this, so she reached around to her pack to find them, but they must have fallen out when she fell off the cliff. She sat up, moaning, and then rolled over onto her hands and knees, then pushed up so she was standing on one leg with the other held up behind her. She carefully put the injured foot onto the ground, and immediately pulled it back up. She tried it again, and this time put a little weight on it. Down she went in a sprawl to the ground. The pain was too much, and it defeated her with stunning ease.

But the pain was not what bothered her the most. It was knowing that she would never be able to finish the race. She had been so close, on the fourth loop of five, through the relentless ascents and descents in the East Tennessee backwoods, and had hoped she would be the first woman to ever finish the world's hardest race. But here she was hurt and alone, and there were only a few other runners left somewhere on the course.

A mixture of rage and despair overwhelmed her.

She was horribly angry at herself for falling off the cliff, and even angrier at the race director for putting such an obstacle into the race. This was supposed to be a race for runners, not mountain climbers! What was he thinking? What was she thinking? Why had she decided she had to do this awful, masochistic race in the first place? Nothing made sense at that moment.

If she could throttle someone, she would, but there was no one there to throttle except herself. So she began shouting at herself, "You stupid idiot! What were you thinking! Look at what all that training got you! You thought you were ready, and look at you now! Nothing but pain! You're a loser, just a loser!" She beat the ground with her fists and wept.

Her tears were falling hot and wet on her cheeks, and dripping into her mouth. The salty taste made her thirsty, so she drank a swallow out of her water bladder, and then forced herself to calm down and take stock.

At least she had fluids left, and some food. She shook her pack to see about how much water was in there. She had filled it at the last water drop, and now it was less than half full. A wet weather stream was rushing through the drainway after all the rain, and it could quench her thirst if she became desperate.

Her food supply was running low, as she was so close to completing a loop and making her way to camp. She did have a few food items tucked away in reserve, though.

She also had some first-aid type emergency items in her pack that might help, and she had one good leg and two good arms. She was smart and determined. She would get out of this mess somehow.

ATTEMPT ONE

Chapter 4: The Adventure Begins

Amanda was a woman on a mission after that day. She read everything she could find on the Internet about the race, and she studiously took notes. She asked all her running friends about it. She looked up the race director on social media and began to follow all of the races he directed. She decided to run one of them, and she had to fly to Tennessee to do it. She did well, coming in as the second woman finisher and getting to meet the race director, laz, afterward.

She had to take time off work to train extra hard, and began asking around about the mystery of how to enter the race. Finally someone gave her some clues, and other information she ferreted out on the Internet. When it came time to enter, she did so at the right time. Only 40 competitors were allowed in every year, but she was confident that her running resume was incredible enough to gain her entry. She felt ready to give this thing a good shot.

When she received her condolence email, she first thought how strange it was to be consoled for getting in the race. Then she started screaming. Robbie came over to see what was wrong, and she threw herself in his arms.

"I'm in! I made it in!" She was shouting in his ear.

"Ouch! Let's turn the volume down a little bit, sweetie," he said, rubbing his ear.

She danced around the living room, then all of a sudden she was overcome with nervousness.

A million doubts flooded her mind and came pouring out. "Oh no! What if I can't do it? How will I prepare? What if I travel all that way and fail? What if I get lost? What if I get hurt and can't do all my other races?" She was suddenly filled with foreboding. She threw herself on the couch and began worrying within five minutes of reading the email.

"You'll figure it out. You can do it, don't worry," said Robbie.

She heard him, but ignored his comforting words. Her thoughts had moved on like a river rushing downstream. "I need to let everybody know I got in," she said excitedly.

"I thought it was a kind of top-secret thing," said Robbie.

"Oh, yeah, well just a few people then," she said, pulling out her phone and eagerly starting to text her family and friends.

After a few days of panic, she began training in earnest, doing more off-trail vertical miles than she had ever attempted before. She ran as much of the ascent as she could, then power-hiked. She threw herself down the descents like a mad woman. She only had three months to train for the hardest race she had ever hoped to do.

She was 40 years old, and had spent most of her life getting an education. Her experiences pursuing advanced degrees in college and only recently working in research had led her to be a list-maker. She made lists for everything she did, and for every day of the week. Focusing on the details was what had made her so successful in achieving her goals.

She used that skill now and began making a list of what to take with her to the race. She had a lot of experience with long distance trail running, so she already had most of her gear. There were a few things she needed to order right away, like new rain gear, and she made a separate list for items to buy. She knew a good rain parka was crucial, because the state park where the race was held had its own weather system, separate from the surrounding area, and past racers had suffered from rain, hail, thunderstorms, sleet, and snow, sometimes all in a three-day period.

She would not be allowed to carry her own watch

(one would be provided with the race time already set), her cell phone, or a navigation device. She had to order her own map of the park online.

About one month before the race, she began making piles of gear all over the living room with pieces of cardboard on top of each pile to label what the pile was for. "Loop One" was her Saturday gear, "Loop Two" was for whenever she started Loop Two, and so forth. She made piles all the way through to "Loop Five," deciding to be hopeful. There was also a pile for "In Camp" gear. If Robbie wanted to sit on the couch, he had to carefully move a stack of gear out of his seat while she frowned menacingly at him.

Her basic gear included a good sports drink to fill her two sturdy water bottles, her best and biggest hydration vest with bladder for water, a lightweight hooded jacket, 2 high lumen head lamps plus one other small hand held light source, compass, hiking poles, leather gloves, several pair of running shoes, a small tent and sleeping bag for when she was in camp, and her new rain gear.

She set out clothing for every loop, including caps and polypro hats, polyester shirts, arm sleeves for warmth, ankle gaiters, shorts, tights, compression knee socks, and underwear. She also had some polyester gloves in each loop's pile.

Her food included gels, bars, chocolate, almond butter and honey to eat on tortillas, the tortillas themselves, and other real food so she wouldn't get sick from too much sugar and start having diarrhea. She hated messy gels and the litter they caused, plus all that sugar upset her stomach, but they were lightweight and easy to consume on the run. A lot of the food she would have to buy when she arrived in Tennessee. She would bag it all up for each loop the night before the race.

There were some emergency items which would fit in the pockets of her hydration vest: her small knife, salt tablets, ibuprofen, anti-chafing gel, a blister kit, a firestarter kit, waterproof matches, a small first-aid kit, sunblock, paracord, a water purification pen, and sunglasses. She planned to carry her map in a zip-locked bag to keep it dry, stashed in a front pocket for easy access. Her compass would be around her neck on a lanyard, but also tucked into a front pocket to keep it from catching on branches. She had duplicates of some items to leave in camp.

She debated whether to carry an emergency bivouac sack or a space blanket, and she tried them both out on a cold night on their balcony. The bivy sack kept her warmer because it was a tube she could get inside, but the space blanket was lighter. She hated to carry any extra weight, but friends had advised her that she should carry one or the other, just in case. Sometimes people got lost and had to spend the night out in the difficult terrain. She couldn't envision needing an emergency cover, though, because she planned to keep running no matter what. She tried to imagine herself hurt and having to spend the night out, and finally threw the bivy sack in the bottom of her pack. It was merely 5.5 ounces more to carry. Later, she pulled it back out.

What was this race going to cost her? There was a ridiculous $1.60 entry fee, an old license plate from Colorado, and a gift of a white dress shirt for the race director. But then the costs of the new gear, the food, the plane ticket, and the rental car, plus other assorted costs, began to mount up. She might have to pay extra for a second suitcase on the airplane.

She pored over the map when it came, and read dozens of race reports from past racers that were posted online. She trolled through the park using Google Earth. Getting a feel for the park vicariously was her top priority, especially since she would not be able to visit it until the actual race week.

She was exhausted most of the time and running on adrenaline. But she loved projects that consumed her entirely, and this race was fast becoming her favorite obsession. It was like falling in love for the very first time; it was all she thought or dreamed about.

ATTEMPT TWO

Chapter 5: Help Is Not Coming

She began screaming as loudly as she could. "Help me! Help! Someone help!" She kept it up for about ten minutes, then became frustrated and gave up.

How was she ever going to get out of the backwoods? Everything seemed so impossible. Would anyone come looking for her? She didn't think she was on the race course any more. And most of the competitors had given up and were in the campground by now, anyway.

She would have to be innovative. Her life up until then had taught her how to figure things out against all odds. There were only three ways out, unless, of course, there was a miracle. One way was to get rescued, which seemed unlikely considering the race's history. A second way was to crawl out, which would be very long and painful. The third way was to somehow make crutches and hop out.

Her hiking poles might work as crutches, but they had fallen out of her pack, and she could not find them. Perhaps she could find a sturdy stick to use to help her get up the hillside and out of the ditch-like ravine to return to the race course. From there, it wasn't too far to the park's boundary where someone would eventually find her. The race had a history of 100% self-extraction, and she definitely didn't want to be the one to mess that up.

She looked about on the forest floor in the late afternoon sunlight and saw a long stick about five feet away. It might work, if it wasn't rotten. She crawled over to it and picked it up. It had a fork at one end that might serve to rest her underarm on. She tried again to stand on one leg, this time using the stick to help her get up. Once she was up, she tried hopping about using the stick. She wrapped one of her arm socks around the forked end to try to make it more comfortable. It might support her, but she didn't know about climbing up a hill with only one leg.

She had no choice but to try it out, so she slowly loped over to the base of the hill and began ascending it, pushing and pulling herself along with the stick and taking smaller steps as the way became steeper. The impulse to put her bad foot down was overwhelming. If only she could use it, she would be out of that hole in no time.

There was a sudden cracking sound. The seemingly sturdy stick gave way and broke into several pieces. She fell forward on the hill, and grabbed at a tree root to keep from falling, but she missed it by a fraction and started sliding down the wet and muddy slope. She managed to keep her bad leg up in the air, and coasted right to the bottom.

She was so tired. All she wanted to do was lie there and sleep a dreamless sleep. She hadn't slept since a few hours of fitful sleep on Friday night before the race, and now it was nearly Sunday night. Her husband's face flitted before her eyes; she missed him terribly. If only he were here with her, he would help her find a way out of this dilemma.

She thought help might come in the morning, but then she remembered the race's fateful slogan, "Help is not coming." A dread seized her heart. There was no way out except through her own fortitude and ingenuity. She would have to figure it out herself.

ATTEMPT ONE

Chapter 6: At the Park

When race week finally arrived, she flew to Knoxville, Tennessee, and rented a car to drive to the park. Robbie was unable to get away from the Emergency Room, so she would be taking care of herself unless she could find someone at the campground who would volunteer to crew her between loops. But maybe she wouldn't need any help. She had always had an independent streak.

At the park, she found the campsite she was sharing with several other people, and someone made a space for her to park her rental car next to her tent. There were a few people she knew from past races, and she was happy to see them. She set up her one person tent, but left the bulk of her gear in the trunk of the car.

It was Monday and the race was on Saturday, so she spent the intervening days scoping out the park by running on the legal trails with other runners who had come early. They had discussions about finding their way through the illegal areas come race day, and spent time on the observation platform of the old fire tower looking out over the horizon and picking out mountain tops and watersheds on the map. The weather was perfect all week with early spring sunshine and 60 degrees. It looked like it would be a great weekend according to the forecast.

One person she was eager to meet was Frozen Ed, the first finisher of the race back in the early days. He continued to come to the race every year and attempt it again, even into his seventies. He finally pulled in on Friday afternoon with his wife, Gail. Immediately, he was surrounded by people who were anxious to greet and meet him. Amanda hung behind, but finally went forward and shook his hand.

"I love your book!" she exclaimed. Frozen Ed had written a popular book about the history of the race, called *Tales From Out There*.

"Thank you! I'm glad you enjoyed it. Do you have it with you so I can sign it for you?"

"Yes, let me go get it!" She ran to her rental car and rummaged through all her gear in the trunk. When she had her hands on it, she ran up the road to Ed.

He wrote inside the cover with an ink pen he pulled out of his shirt pocket, and returned the book to her. She thanked him, and walked down to her car, eagerly opening the book to read his inscription before she even got there.

"To Amanda. Look out for the Bad Thing! See you

Out There! Frozen Ed."

She wondered what the Bad Thing was, and sort of remembered there was some saying about the Bad Thing in something she had read about the race. She knew there was a nasty mountain called the Bad Thing, so maybe that was what he was referring to.

Someone was standing beside her car when she came down the road. It was a young woman with long, blonde hair tied loosely in a ponytail. She said her name was Emily, and she was looking for a last-minute space to set up her tent. She asked Amanda if there was any room at her campsite. Her family would be coming out, but they wouldn't show up until after the race started, so it was only her.

Amanda said, "Maybe you could set up down there," and pointed to an area below a rocky outcrop behind the campsite that wasn't technically part of the campsite. "It's nice and flat anyway. I don't think the park cares so much if you are off the official tent pad this weekend. The campground is totally full. Maybe I can move my car up a little bit and Russ can move his backwards some. But if it won't fit, you'll have to unload your gear and move your car down to the parking lot by the picnic pavilion."

Amanda thought to herself that the younger woman should have arrived that morning or earlier in the week, or asked for a space online before coming out. It would be tricky to fit her car into the already cramped parking area.

Emily said, "Oh, that's okay. I will unload my gear and use that spot by the rocks. You don't have to move your cars. I don't mind parking at the bottom."

Amanda watched out of the corner of her eye as Emily trotted down to the area below the rocks and began setting up her tent. She didn't appear to be having a problem, so she didn't offer to help her. Emily hauled all her gear down to her tent and dutifully drove her car to the parking lot at the picnic pavilion. When she came hiking back up, she attempted a conversation with Amanda.

"So, have you checked in yet?"

"No, laz is not here yet," said Amanda with irritation sitting on the edge of her voice.

"Oh, well, I guess we can't look at the map yet, then," said a dejected Emily.

"Of course not," said Amanda. She didn't want to spend hours answering this younger woman's stupid questions. She needed to prepare her food for the race.

"Have you been out there yet?" The young woman

persisted in trying to talk to her.

"Yes, but only on the easy, candyass trails," replied Amanda. She looked Emily up and down and thought she looked like a fast runner. She was of medium height with not a shred of extra flab on her. Her bare legs and arms were strong and muscular. She had a curious habit of always looking off into the distance like she was afraid to make eye contact.

Introvert, thought Amanda.

"So you're Amanda Bivens, the famous ultrarunner? You won the Top of the Tetons Trail 100 race last fall? And beat all the men by an hour?" Emily hurriedly asked.

Amanda was surprised that Emily knew anything about her. She pulled her shoulders back and smiled. "Yes, that's me!"

"I'm so glad to meet you. I wish I was as fast as you. What have you raced recently?" asked Emily.

"Well, I placed third in the women's division in the Western Wildcat Ultra, and fourth place overall in the Tooth Gnasher 100," said Amanda. "Not to brag or anything."

Emily looked properly in awe. "I only started ultrarunning three years ago. I haven't done too badly, but nothing like your finishes. But this race has been eating at me for the last year. I only live about thirty minutes from here," Emily confided, all in a rush.

"Oh?" Amanda asked. "So have you been training out here?"

"Yes, of course, every chance I get," said Emily.

"But only on the legal trails?" asked Amanda, suspiciously.

"Oh, I would never cheat," said Emily. "But I have been able to spend a lot of time out there, more than most people, so maybe that will help me."

"I think it might. But you have to have speed, too. And know how to navigate well. And not be afraid of anything, or of trashing your body," cautioned Amanda.

"Navigation is an issue for me, for sure. I couldn't find my way out of my back yard when I started trying to learn how to use a map and compass," said Emily, looking off into the trees.

"I'm pretty good at it. I have been using a map and compass since I was about thirteen. Learned how from my Mom. She was a back country emergency responder. I love finding my way," confessed Amanda.

"Maybe you will let me stay with you for the first loop, then?" Emily asked hopefully.

"I don't know. It depends on how fast you are. I plan to get in the lead pack and hang on," said Amanda, starting to rustle around in the trunk of her car. She wasn't sure she wanted to commit to running with someone she didn't know.

"Okay, well, I'll look for you tomorrow and see if I can keep up," said Emily shyly. She began to walk down to her tent to organize her gear, when the race director, laz, arrived in his white rental van, waving out the window at a few people.

"Laz is here!" People were yelling happily.

Amanda grabbed her map and a few other things and took off up the road to be among the first to greet laz and get checked in. She looked behind her, and saw Emily walking to her tent. She must have decided to organize her gear and check in later.

Amanda was itching to see the master map and race directions so she could mark the race route on her own map. It would be the first time any of the runners knew the exact race route, because it changed somewhat every year.

Maybe, if she hurried, she could snag a good spot at the picnic table. Later, the race's gregarious chicken cook, scRitch, would be roasting the famous "digitally prepared" chicken quarters on the grill, with barbeque sauce slathered on with his bare hands, and she hoped to try it out.

ATTEMPT TWO

Chapter 7: Never Give Up

Something inside her wouldn't let her give up. It was a hard little knot of defiance that welled up in her gut. She clung to it.

She thought she would try again to climb out of the ravine after she rested for a short while. She lay still and watched as dusk melted the world around her into shadows. Night was upon her, so she pulled out her head lamp, but kept it turned off while she rested. Her ankle throbbed and her forehead burned, and her worries filled her mind.

She worried that her family was anxious about her. She worried that she would never make it out of there alive. Her ankle might be beyond repair if she did make it out, and she might never run again.

She worried that the snake might slither down the hill to where she was lying helpless as a baby. Good grief! It was too early in the year for snakes! But she remembered that the two weeks leading up to the race had been sunny and warm, so it wasn't a huge surprise that she had encountered one. She also remembered that rattlesnakes did not hiss, so it must have been another kind of snake.

Snakes had always been her number one fear, until lately. The story of the Bad Thing had frightened her very deeply. What if the Bad Thing found her? It would sense her fears and attack. She felt so defenseless and alone.

It would soon be nighttime, when all the evil things creeped and crawled and flew, seeking hapless prey in the deep mountainous terrain. She became immensely afraid.

She started yelling and wailing again out of desperation. "Help! HELP! Help me!" But no one answered, and no one came to help.

There was nothing to do but get up again and attempt to free herself from the clutches of the ravine. She was determined to hop, crawl, tumble, and get up again until she made it out, or died trying.

ATTEMPT ONE

Chapter 8: Everything Changes

When she arrived at the race headquarters' campsite, she discovered there was a lot of work to do before she could get checked in. All of laz's race gear had to be unloaded from the van and carried to the picnic table. The firewood had to be unloaded from the truck. Luckily, the "Taj Mahal," a big, white, picnic table tent that was donated every year, was already set up. The numerous packages of semi-frozen chicken quarters were being unloaded, too, but laz put a stop to that. He only wanted one package out at a time, and the rest were wrapped up in a tarp to stay cold inside his van. Then laz said no one could check in until he got the 30+ years of license plate donations strung up on ropes all around the campsite. That would take a while because he insisted that only he could do it right.

Amanda enjoyed reconnecting with old friends and making some new ones while helping with all of the work. There was some discussion about the new goings-on at the state park. The park evidently had surplus funds, and workers were busily expanding the campground. The trees behind the race headquarters' campsite had been cut down and removed, and gravel was piled up ready to be smoothed out into new campsites. It looked like at least three new campsites were being put in behind headquarters. Electric was being run to all the campsites in the campground, too.

Laz made it clear that he was not certain he liked these changes. The worst of it was that the Yellow Gate was being dismantled. The rocks had been cracking and falling off the pillars for years, but now they had been completely removed and stacked up on the side of the road. The Yellow Gate looked naked. Evidently the gate was going to be moved up the jeep road past the new campsites, to block the entrance to the jeep road and the back country farther up. This would allow people access to the new campsites.

Laz and RawDog had been rock wall builders in their younger days and had always hoped to be the ones to rebuild the Yellow Gate pillars if the park ever decided to do that. Now Danger (RawDog's eldest son), who owned a landscaping and rock wall building company, had hopes of rebuilding the new pillars, and had been talking to park rangers about getting the job.

Laz was moping about, grumbling like an old man about how nothing ever stays the same.

One of the veterans of the race spoke up and said, "Yeah, but you change the race course every year!

So why be upset about this?"

Laz kept mumbling about how nothing was ever good enough, and somebody was always wrecking things. The runners were looking at each other with raised eyebrows, nodding their heads in agreement, but really they were thinking about how laz changed the race every year to make it more difficult.

This year it looked like the start and finish could still be held at the Yellow Gate, sans pillars, but next year the race would start and end about an eighth of a mile up the jeep road.

Everyone joked about how laz would have to get a golf cart to access the new gate location quickly from the old headquarters' campsite, or else he would have to move headquarters way up the road to the last new campsite, which would effectively limit his communication with the other campers. Who would be able to hear the conch shell being blown to signify one more hour until the race began? Perhaps loudspeakers would become necessary in the future. Or someone suggested using the golf cart to let laz ride around the campground while blowing the conch shell. Kyle, RawDog's youngest son, said he could design a fancy sign to put on the front of the golf cart that said, "lazmobile."

Laz was also secretly upset about how far he would

have to walk to the bathroom in the future. "I already almost can't make it down there as it is," he confided in RawDog.

He had to spend all his time at the Yellow Gate for three days and nights during the race. For nature calls and showers he had to carve out some time and get someone to watch the gate while he was gone. He and the Yellow Gate were attached by an invisible umbilical cord that limited his every move.

RawDog suggested he use some of the race funds to rent his own personal port-a-potty. They could get Kyle to make another sign that said "laz only. Stay out, you morons!" That way, laz would have his own bathroom and wouldn't get so upset about going in the bathhouse and sitting in pee someone had sprinkled all over the toilet seat.

At last the famous chicken was cooked and some people got to eat. Amanda was first in line for her piece. She had expected it to be frozen in the middle, but it was cooked perfectly. She also helped herself to some beans from the giant can set in the campfire. She sat down to eat in the first available chair by the fire. Life was good.

Shortly after that, she was allowed to check in, and get her race bib and race instructions. Laz was glad to see her. He told her to be careful. He had a wicked grin with perfect teeth surrounded by an overgrowth of graying-blonde beard and thinning blonde and gray hair had that had grown out to below shoulder length now that he stopped shaving his head. He rubber-banded it at the base of his neck in a long rat tail. He was always quirky with funny responses that could be misconstrued as slightly evil, but everyone liked him.

Most of the other competitors soon showed up to check in. They all crowded around the picnic table to peer at the master map. Amanda snagged a prime seat right in the middle, and she carefully marked the route on her own map using a yellow highlighter pen.

There was a lot of discussion about the new changes in the race route, and she listened intently, trying to absorb as much knowledge as she could. Frozen Ed sat next to her, and everyone wanted to hear his thoughts about the changes.

Later, as she was leaving to go to bed, she saw Emily coming up to get checked in. "Hi!" they both said.

Amanda thought it had taken Emily a long time to come up and get checked in. She kept walking down to her campsite, thinking that Emily was probably so slow that she would never see her in the race.

She crawled into her tent and set her alarm clock for 6 a.m., although she had no idea when the race would start. If it was late, she wanted to be up at 6 anyway to get proper hydration and nutrition. It could start any time after midnight. There was no way to know. The race time was a closely guarded secret—just another method of torturing the runners.

After she got tucked into her sleeping bag and got nice and warm, she had to get up again and go pee. She had forgotten to brush her teeth, so she did that too. By then she was wide awake and couldn't return to bed, so she put her jacket on and went up to the Yellow Gate in her jammies to listen to the stories around the fire.

The chicken chef, scRitch, was done cooking chicken and was telling the story about when he had run the race back at the beginning of its history, gotten lost, and had to spend the night in the mountains with another runner under a space blanket. It was a funny story, and people were listening and laughing. His voice droned up and over the campground and out into the darkness of the forest, where the Bad Thing was eagerly waiting for the runners to enter its territory.

ATTEMPT TWO

Chapter 9: A New Idea

She thought that her missing hiking poles might be useful in helping her climb out of the ravine, so she shone her headlight all around and tried to find them by crawling and clawing through piles of wet leaves. Something metallic glinted in her headlamp's bright light, and she moved towards it. There were both her poles, lying crisscrossed in the dead leaves by a tree. A wave of relief washed over her.

What if she unscrewed them, raised them up as high as her underarms, and tried to use them as crutches? Would they be sturdy enough? She twisted them up until they were the proper length to fit under her arms, but she worried they might collapse if she wasn't vigilant.

Slowly, she pulled herself off the ground by holding onto the two poles, and placed the tops of them under her arm pits. She had never used crutches, so she had to think for a minute how to use them. She remembered watching a child with one leg using crutches on a playground. He would move the crutches forward of his body, lean, then glide his leg forward. He fell down a lot, especially if he turned quickly to chase a ball, but he got right back up and never cried. She would try to be half as fearless as him.

With her bad leg held up behind her, she moved the hiking poles forward, leaned, and tried to glide her legs forward. It was hard because the hiking poles were not as sturdy as crutches, and didn't have much support for her hands. She lurched around to get the feel of it. This would work better than the stick, she thought, but the tops of the poles poked her underarms and hurt, so they would need some padding. Also, if she fell, she worried that her hurt ankle would hit something and get torn up more.

She hopped over to her pack and sat down next to it. What had she brought with her that she could use? She looked at the two sturdy water bottles in the front pockets of her hydration vest. If she cut holes in the sides of those, she could pop them onto the tops of the hiking poles and they would make good underarm rests. She could wrap her arm sleeves around them for padding.

What else would help her with self-extraction? There was some duct tape, some paracord, her knife, and her extra clothing. If she could pad her ankle, and maybe build some kind of makeshift splint, she might be able to protect it. She wished she had an Ace bandage, but she couldn't carry everything for every eventuality. She wrapped her extra polyester shirt around her ankle and tied it off with the shirt sleeves. Then she tried to stretch out one of her ankle gaiters over it all, but was unsuccessful.

Her ankle had swollen to twice its size, and it hurt to touch it. She needed to elevate and ice it, but that wasn't happening. Moaning as she touched it, she felt morose all over again about not completing the race. Her worst fear assaulted her. Would she ever run again?

It was time to stay focused on her task. She still had her tights on and her long socks, so they would provide some padding around her ankle region. She needed to make something to immobilize her ankle, so she found a sapling and used her knife to cut off some small branches. She roughly cut them to the right length and fashioned a kind of splint by sticking several of the pieces of wood on either side of her ankle, using the duct tape and paracord to keep them there, and making sure the whole contraption was not too tight. Now her ankle was enclosed in a protective shell, so at least if she bashed it against something, the splint might provide some protection. She left her wet shoe on, although her foot felt very tight and swollen inside it. The shoe might provide some added protection.

The narrow gully she lay in was very dark now. She couldn't see her hand in front of her face unless she used her headlamp. She had a back-up headlamp in case the first one died, so she wasn't too worried about keeping it turned on.

She decided to keep screaming as long as she could, and wore herself out with it. Her voice became hoarse. She took a few sips of water from her water bladder, but conserved most of it for the next day. She wasn't very hungry, but had a piece of pre-cooked, thick bacon for the protein and fat.

She decided to sleep a while if she could, and then try to escape again at first light. Her pain level had lessened some once she put the splint on her ankle, but she rummaged around in her pack and found her acetaminophen and took some. Ibuprofen upset her stomach, so she never carried it.

The chill of night seeped into the forest and into her bones, and she was getting colder by the minute. The threat of hypothermia was very real in these conditions.

She remembered her piece of fatwood and her

lighter. She had hiked out in the woods that winter and found an old, dead pine tree lying on the ground. It had been lying there for years, and the soft wood on the outside had rotted away. She reached down and pulled out a long piece of the glistening, dark orange heartwood. She smelled it, and the turpentine smell of the concentrated pine pitch was unmistakable. She had taken home a large piece, then chopped it up to use to start fires. She had stuck a piece of it into her race pack. Her heavy heart said a prayer of thanks that now she could use it to beat the wet conditions.

She gathered up some dead branches that had fallen and were hanging in the lower tree branches, and also found some dead branches lying on the ground with tiny twigs sticking up that had not touched the wet ground. There were also many dead lower branches still attached to living trees. The branches had died without enough sunlight reaching them in the deep forest. She snapped those off to use for her fire, and soon had enough kindling.

Next, she cleared the wet debris off a circle of ground, and dug down into the soil a little ways with a rock until it felt drier. She made a flat place for her fire. She pulled out her fatwood and her lighter, and laid the piece of fatwood on the ground. Splinters sticking out from the end of it lit easily with her lighter, and the fatwood produced a steady flame. Then she added the smallest tinder she had found, gradually adding bigger pieces. The fire was smoky at first, but then it burned brightly. Pretty soon, she had a cheerful flame to warm her hands.

She remembered her emergency bivouac sack, and pulled it out of the bottom of her pack and out of its tight draw-string sack, wondering how people ever stuffed them back inside those little orange sacks. She wrapped the bivy around herself, not bothering to crawl inside. She was exhausted, and lay down a little ways from her fire, tucked her legs up, and immediately passed out.

ATTEMPT ONE

Chapter 10: The Best Laid Plans

The race didn't start with a gunshot or a countdown, but on a wave of exhaled breaths when laz lit his cigarette at exactly 5:37 a.m. Everyone began walking and running up the jeep road in the pre-dawn darkness and chill. Family and friends standing on the embankment were hollering out the names of their loved ones. The media people were standing both beside the road and in the road snapping pictures and shooting video footage.

Amanda snuck around the gate, which never opened for the start, and poked her way through the crowd, saying, "Excuse me!" to get through to the front. There were two fast men at the front, and she decided to stick close to them as they climbed the first mountain. They made it to the first book in record time, and she tore out her book page and continued following them, feeling certain they knew the way.

As they were crashing down Jaquemate Hill in the morning fog, she was somewhat slower on the descent and couldn't keep up with them. She didn't really know them, and didn't have an agreement with them to stay with them. They took off into the dense fog as if they had passed through a door and closed it behind them.

She could hear the other runners above her noisily thrashing down the mountainside.

"Do I wait or do I try to catch the leaders?" Amanda was unsure what to do. She decided to try to catch the two leaders, and tore down the mountainside like a chipmunk trying to get to its hole before the hawk swooped down.

After five or ten minutes of this, and not finding the two men who were ahead of her, and not hearing the pack behind her, she realized she might have travelled off course. She pulled out her map and compass and tried to figure out where she was. From past experience in other races, she knew the best thing to do was to return to where she had known where she was and figure it out from there, but that would mean climbing back up that mountain. No way was she going to do that.

So she decided to move in a northeast direction and try to hook up with some of the main pack of runners descending the mountain.

She made it to the corner of the park by luck, and ran into Frozen Ed and several others, including Emily.

"Thank God!" she exclaimed when she saw Ed.

Here was someone who knew the way.

She joined in with the group and began following Ed as he flawlessly navigated through the landmarks. A few of the competitors decided to travel faster, and took off ahead of them.

Amanda decided to stay right behind Ed so she could hear his descriptions of where they were and where they were going, and look over his shoulder at the map when he pulled it out. Emily was right there next to her every step of the way, listening and observing. Sometimes it seemed like the two of them were competing for Ed's attention, asking him questions simultaneously and practically pushing each other out of the way. Amanda was starting to get annoyed with this young woman.

Amanda knew she could run faster than both of them. But it would be wise to stay with someone who knew the course. Her plan to stay with the leaders had been incinerated when she got lost. All it took was slowing down or losing focus for one minute. Now she would have to use Plan B, which was to learn the terrain this year and come back next year with more knowledge and fire in her gut.

She was extremely determined, but unfortunately, there was no guarantee of getting in the race next year, especially if she had a poor performance this year.

ATTEMPT TWO

Chapter 11: The Bad Thing Cometh

She dreamed of the Bad Thing coming to carry her away to its nest. It grabbed her hair and drooled on her cheeks. Its bulging eyes bored holes into her soul. She shook her head violently to get it off. As it clawed her face, she clawed herself awake.

Stunned, she sat up, shivering. Her fire was still burning merrily. She checked her watch, and she had only been asleep for 15 minutes.

There were strange, rustling sounds in the tree above her. She looked up, and wondered sleepily what it was.

Shrill noises pierced her ears. It sounded like two women talking noisily to each other.

"Hello?" she said, hoping someone was there.

She turned on her headlamp and began casting the light around the bottom of the ravine, then in the tops of the trees. She could see nothing moving at all. Her nightmare of the Bad Thing was still hovering about, and she began to feel more scared than she ever had in her life. She needed to get out of the ravine in the worst way.

So she yanked off the bivy sack, clumsily rolled it up and tried to stuff it back into its little draw-string sack. It was futile, and she angrily threw the tiny orange sack on the ground. She rolled up the bivy sack tightly and pushed it through the loops on the back of her pack, put her pack on, grabbed her poles, and gingerly stood up. She began lurching up the incline, but soon the steepness was too much for her. She would have to crawl out. Sticking her poles in the back of her pack, she crawled, using her elbows and knees, and holding her hurt leg up in the air behind her so it wouldn't drag. She pulled herself up bit by bit, and thought she might make it. She was huffing and puffing, and moaning loudly.

Suddenly a dark shape swooped down from the trees right above her. She heard a high-pitched shriek, "Whoooooooooooooooo!"

She flattened her body to the ground and held her breath. The dark wings passed over her and flapped up into a tree at the top of the ravine. She lay there trembling. Was it going to come back?

A whooshing *sound descended upon her, and an immense weight landed on her pack and head, pushing her face into the dirt.*

"Whub," *she said, making a sick noise like an*

antelope hit by a charging lion.

The thing began yanking her hair in every direction, and screaming and clucking. Its talons were razor sharp, and several plunged into her scalp where it met the top of her neck, causing a maddening, burning pain to run from her head to her toes.

It was exactly like her nightmare. Was it the Bad Thing, this time really coming to carry her up to its nest to feed its young?

At first she lay still, in shock, and hoping it would fly away, but it continued pulling on her hair and caterwauling like a woman giving birth. She couldn't just lay there doing nothing, and started to twist her torso and slap up at it with her hands, yelling, "Get off of me!"

The weight of the creature and her own crazy thrashing movements caused her to slide down to the bottom of the ravine where she had first started her climb.

The Bad Thing still hung on to her head.

Was it going to try to lift her to the trees above?

ATTEMPT ONE

Chapter 12: Irish Tales

When they arrived at the Memorial Cairn, someone was there ahead of them. It was a small, dark-haired, middle-aged man, and he was folding his book page into his pack with both hands and munching on a granola bar hanging out of his mouth.

He spit his granola bar out into his left hand when he saw them, and called out, "How's it going?"

"Hey, Tadhg!" said Ed, happy to see an old friend.

"What's his name?" Emily whispered to Amanda.

"I don't know. Tige? Like tiger without the *e-r*?" Amanda whispered back, unsure.

"Ladies, this is Tadhg, an old Irish buddy of mine. Tadhg, this is Amanda and Emily."

Tadhg held out his right hand to shake hands with each of them. "Name is Tadhg, spelled *T-a-d-h-g*," he said, as if he had overheard them whispering. "It's an ancient name from medieval times, I tell ya. It was handed down through the years to every first-born male, including me Da and me," said Tadhg, shoving another bite of granola bar into his mouth between sentences.

"Tige, with a long *i*?" said Emily in a sweet voice.

"Yes, but ya say it like this: T-*uh*-ige. The Irish way," said Tadhg, laughing.

Amanda was at the Memorial Cairn adding a stone to the pile. The Memorial Cairn was a large landmark of rocks piled up, that had been built by friends to honor past veterans of the race who have passed away. Every runner was supposed to add a rock as they passed by.

Amanda was surprised to see small white chunks of something lying on top and in niches in the rocks of the Cairn. She curiously reached out to pick one piece up. Tadhg descended upon her, yelling, "No, don't touch them!"

It was too late. Amanda held one in the palm of her hand, and turned it over into her other hand, wondering what it was. It appeared to be a chunk of bone.

"*Ugh*!" She had an image of her hand holding a nasty, decaying body, and quickly dropped the bone.

Tadhg said, "Those are the bones of the Bad Thing."

"What?" Amanda sputtered. "What is this Bad Thing I keep hearing about?"

"Have ya not heard the tale of the Bad Thing then?"

"Noooooooo," said Amanda, with a question in her voice.

"Why, he's been around here for years and years, now don't look so shocked. His bones are here, ya can be sure, right I am. But at night they kind of fuse back together to make a fearsome creature." Tadhg was standing in front of the three of them now, telling his story with a profound look on his face.

"He swoops down on frightened runners and attacks with his knife-like talons, yes he does," he mimicked such an attack with his hands slicing the air.

"If the racers are afraid of anything, he can sense their fears and absorb their fright to make himself even bigger and more fearful, I'm tellin' ya the honest truth. He has an enormous wingspan." He stretched his arms out wide and puffed up his chest.

"He tries to grab people by the hair with his long, yellow talons, and it's shocking, but he tries to carry them up into the trees to his gigantic nest to feed his mate and little ones. His ugly face has bulging eyes and long feathers, with a leering, slobbering grin, so it does. Ya don't want to be afraid out here, I tell ya."

Amanda felt an unwonted prickle of adrenaline riding up the back of her neck, and she gingerly picked up the chunk of bone and placed it on a flat rock on the Cairn, while Tadhg watched, sighing and frowning.

"I wisht ya had na touched it. The Bad Thing has your scent now," said Tadhg, in an ominous tone.

"Oh, you made all that up. Those are just old 'possum bones," scoffed Amanda, smacking her hands together to remove the feel of the bone.

"But Amanda," whispered a trembling Emily. "What if he didn't?"

Tadhg was not smiling. Ed's forehead crinkled with worry lines, and he started heading out to the water drop. "Let's get going. There's nothing to fret about. It's just one of Tadhg's stories," he said, forcing a laugh.

"Now I tell ya, me Grandda was the story teller, not me," retorted Tadhg.

He began a new story as they ran down the dirt road to the water drop. "Did I ever tell ya the one about the one-eyed red dragon named Bedaugh, who

terrorized me great great great grandda's village?
Me grandda used to tell it to us young'uns at his
knee and scare the wits out of us. I think he was
havin a bit of fun, but us young'uns couldna sleep at
night, and do ya know what I did? I was just a wee
young lad, mind ya, and I was so scared that I took
me blanket and slept in the closet," said Tadhg in
his melodious voice.

Amanda could almost imagine a violin wailing from
within the forest background as his voice rose and
fell.

After refilling their water bottles and bladders, they
ran together on a jeep track as a group now, with Ed
and Amanda in front and Tadhg and Emily behind.
Tadhg continued telling stories all the way to the
next book's hiding place. The others didn't mind
too much because it took their minds off their pain,
and listening to Tadhg was like listening to music in
the forest.

But Amanda, though outwardly tough and
determined, had thoughts of the Bad Thing coming
down out of the trees and grabbing her by her hair.
She didn't believe a word of Tadhg's story, but she
yanked her cap out of a pocket and pulled it down
over her hair, as if that would somehow stop the
monster.

ATTEMPT TWO

Chapter 13: Fight!

She tried to find something to hit it with. A big rock would do. But reaching out and around her body, she came up empty-handed.

She thought if she rolled over, maybe she could grab it, but then she might miss and it would attack her face and abdomen with its claws.

She tried anyway, but its weight held her down.

Her hands were still thrashing about, and one of them hit something hard. A tree limb was suddenly in her grasp. She tried to use it to hit the monster off her head, but only smashed her ear in the process. The creature began beating its massive wings, and she feared it would lift her off the ground.

She desperately pulled out her pocketknife, opened it, and began slashing at the creature's legs on her head. She slashed and poked, and even though the angle of her attack was difficult, she made contact, but the monster grabbed her hand in its mouth and bit her viciously.

"Ouch!" she screamed. She dropped the knife into

the dark cesspool of the ravine.

Finally, she had had enough. She reached up behind her head with both hands, determined to grab it. She wrapped her fingers around its legs and yanked upwards as hard as she could. The suddenness of her decision surprised the creature, and she succeeded in loosening its grip. Before it could re-attach, she yanked again, and it came loose, but it was biting angrily at her hands. She sat up quickly, and slung the monster against a nearby tree. She let go, and its head hit the tree bark with a hard thunk. The creature landed in a pile of feathers at the base of the tree, and fluttered its wings feebly. There were a few clacking and clucking noises, then it grew silent, and there was no more movement. She breathed hard, still fearful; then she realized she had killed the Bad Thing.

ATTEMPT ONE

Chapter 14: The Dark Tunnel

When the four of them made it to the tunnel beneath the old, abandoned maximum security prison, Ed and Tadhg splashed right through the creek running through it without any hesitation.

Amanda followed, but then heard Emily yell, "No!" She turned and looked back, wondering what had happened. She wanted to move on through the tunnel and get out of the clutching darkness and back into the light. Emily should be able to take care of herself. Then she heard Emily wailing, "Amanda!"

Amanda sighed, and looked behind her. Emily was definitely not coming. She stomped through the stream to the beginning where Emily stood wringing her hands.

"I can't go in there!" Emily cried.

"Why not? What's the matter? Amanda asked her in an exasperated voice.

"I have claustrophobia!" I can't do it! Isn't there any way around it?" Emily moaned.

"No, you have to go through this storm drain on

every loop. You knew that when you entered the race, didn't you?" Amanda tried to control her rising irritation with this young lady.

"Yes, but I figured I would conquer my fears when I got here," said Emily contritely.

"Well, now's the time. Let's get a move on and catch up to Ed and Tadhg!" Amanda was yelling, almost in her face now.

"I can't," balked Emily. "What if the Bad Thing is waiting for us inside?"

"There's no such thing as a Bad Thing!" Amanda stomped around a bit on the bank and shook off some of her anger.

She thought about leaving this scaredy cat behind. Then she suddenly had a plan, and said, "I knew you were a wuss the first time I saw you. Little scared wuss of a thing. Just look at you! What a pansy!" She had her hands on her hips, and was looking Emily up and down with scorn written all over her face.

"I'm NOT a wuss! You don't know anything about me. You don't know what awful things I've had to overcome in my life!" Emily was yelling now.

"Then come on and get over this. It's just one more thing. Get your ass moving," Amanda demanded in her best personal trainer voice.

Emily stomped into the tunnel's dark opening, saying, "Leave me alone!"

As soon as she was barely inside, she turned around and started to exit back to the light.

"No!" Amanda said, grabbing her arm. "You're in here now, just keep going!"

"No, I have to get out!" cried Emily, yanking her arm away.

"Let's do it together. Here, take my hand," coaxed Amanda, worried if Emily exited the tunnel, she would never goad her inside again.

Emily reluctantly took Amanda's hand.

Amanda said, "Frozen Ed says the tunnel is about 300 steps long. We'll count them as we go." She began jogging through the creek deeper and deeper into the tunnel, dragging Emily behind her. Their headlamps lit up the space before them. They counted loudly, "1, 2, 3, 4, 5…"

When they had counted 84 steps, they could see a small circle of light at the other end of the tunnel. "Now imagine yourself there within that circle of light," said Amanda.

Amanda stuck out her free hand and touched the uneven rock surface of the cold and slimy wall, and then quickly pulled her hand back, thinking about the stories of the copperhead snakes as big around as her legs that inhabited this old storm drain. The tunnel was saturated with an evil aura. It was as if the prison walls above had absorbed the horrors and misery experienced by the prisoners, and it was oozing down into the tunnel below.

She sloshed through the stream to the other end, keeping her eye on the ever widening circle of light, with Emily in tow, still counting the steps to the light.

When they reached the end of the storm drain, they let go of each other's hand, and stared at a vertical wall they would need to climb to exit the tunnel. They unanimously decided to continue through deeper water to a safer place to climb out on the left.

"You did it!" said Amanda, offering her hand for a high five.

Emily slapped her hand, and said, "Thanks!"

The two of them ran to the book location and ripped out their pages. As soon as she had her page, Emily tore off up the next steep mountain, which strangely enough was called the Bad Thing by the competitors.

Amanda stood there for a few seconds, wondering if the mountain called the Bad Thing was the home of the monster called the Bad Thing. Then she realized she would be all alone if she didn't keep up, so she ran after Emily and climbed up the never-ending mountain that appeared to touch the sky.

ATTEMPT TWO

Chapter 15: Resurrection

After the attack by the Bad Thing, she rolled onto her hands and knees and started violently retching. Everything she had eaten in the last few hours came up and spewed out. Stress always made her throw up. She felt desperately exhausted. She took some electrolytes and drank some water.

She found her knife and picked it up, just in case she needed it again. Then she watched the creature lying motionless on the ground for a while, anxiously waiting to see if it would get back up and fly away. It didn't appear to be able to, so she struggled over to her pack and found her first-aid kit. She rubbed a couple of alcohol wipes on the back of her head and her neck where the monster had dug in its talons, and bandaged up her hand where it bit her. The puncture wounds on her head and neck did not bleed much, so she left them uncovered.

Her fire needed attention, so she added some tiny branches. The little flames lit up the area around her, and she was grateful for the light.

All of a sudden, the lump of the Bad Thing began

to twitch and make feeble sounds. She was horrified, and scooted behind a big tree to watch. She cowered behind it, holding her pocketknife in one hand in case it attacked her again. Her heart was thumping madly in her chest, and she couldn't breathe.

The creature fluttered one of its enormous wings. She heard it flapping and could barely see its dark shape moving from the light of her fire. It gave out a pitiful squawk, then suddenly righted itself. It shook its wings and clucked and squealed angrily. Then its massive form lifted off the ground into the darkness that permeated the ravine. It passed above her like the shadow of a blimp, but moving swiftly away.

She let out her breath, not realizing she had been holding it. The Bad Thing was still alive, but it had flown away. Maybe it wouldn't return, since she had fought it off and knocked it out. Still, she anxiously hid behind the tree for a while to see if it was coming back.

She needed something to eat, as her blood sugar had plummeted down like a seesaw as her fear rose up. She had a small pouch filled with pure maple sugar and ginger, and the sweetness might perk her up, so she crawled back to her pack and found it and sucked it down. She was still hungry, *so she pulled out a chocolate energy bar and chewed bites of it. Some more sips of water helped it slide down into her stomach where she hoped the calories would help her face the coming day. It would be daylight soon. She sat by her little fire, clutching her opened pocketknife, then gave in to the giant hand of sleep pushing her down to the ground, where she passed out again.*

ATTEMPT ONE

Chapter 16: Misery and Confusion

They didn't see their fellow runners until they made it to the Eye of the Needle. The book was missing from the rock ledge where it was supposed to be sitting. Ed and Tadhg were scurrying about in the underbrush, looking for the book.

"Maybe someone threw it into the briers instead of returning it to its proper place," said Ed.

"We'll find it," yelled Amanda positively, joining them in the search.

Emily stood under the overhang and looked around. She saw something behind a big rock, and bent over to pick it up.

"I found it!" she screamed.

"Where was it?" yelled Tadhg, running over to her.

"Right there behind that rock. Someone must have wanted to confuse us and pitched it over there," said Emily.

"Good job!" said Ed, as he thrashed his way through the briers and up to the group.

Emily beamed, and opened the zip-locked bag that

held the book, then tore out her page first. The others ripped out their pages, and hurriedly stuffed bites of cookies and energy bars into their mouths.

"Time for the Zipline!" said Ed. "I'm not sure why laz named it that," he said thoughtfully. "It makes no sense, because the name makes you think of flying down a zip line, but you can't really zip down this mountain. It is more like a horrible obstacle course. I think laz gave it a sarcastic name. It really should be named Misery and Confusion."

"Misery and Confusion?" exclaimed Tadhg. "Why, that calls for a drink of Irish whiskey!" He pulled out a flask from inside his jacket and took a long slug. "I feel better already!"

He passed the flask to Ed, who shook his head and said, "I'd love to try it after the race, but not right now."

Emily took a wee little sip, and Amanda took a giant gulp. She felt suddenly woozy, and the whiskey burned all the way down the Zipline.

.

ATTEMPT TWO

Chapter 17: A New Day

She awoke to fingers of golden light filtering through the trees into the ravine where she lay. One touched her closed eyes, and she opened them quickly, half expecting to be attacked again.

The knife was still in one hand, her fingers wrapped around it loosely. She had never let go. She checked her watch and was surprised to see that she had only slept about thirty minutes, but she felt refreshed. Her fire had died down to coals and a few sputtering flames.

There was no sign of the Bad Thing anywhere. A few birds were calling nearby, cheerfully singing in the new day. She yawned, and stretched her arms out, wincing at the pain in her back and hip. Then she reached down and felt her ankle. It was so swollen that it didn't really hurt any more, but she knew it would once she began dragging and bumping it along behind her.

She found herself worrying about everything again. Her family was uppermost in her mind, and she wondered if they were looking for her. She was very anxious about her ability to walk or run again. Then there were smaller, prickly worries that caused her emotional pain. One thing she couldn't understand was why her friend had left her behind when they had agreed to do the race together. Did the young woman really dislike her that much? She had felt some friction between them, but speculated that it was due to their mutual competitive drives. She had hoped they could be friends and supportive of each other's efforts, but that didn't seem to have worked out.

It was going to be another horrible day. She had to shake off her worries and prepare for the misery ahead.

ATTEMPT ONE

Chapter 18: Not Gonna Win Today

They made good time as they travelled the remainder of the loop. They made the descent to the forks of the river, then climbed up the torturous Big Hell to the capstones area, then made a frenzied run to the road leading up to the Yellow Gate. The four of them arrived at the same time, and touched the gate together, smiling.

Laz stuck out his lower lip and said, "Now there are no ties in this race, so who is going to claim last place?"

"I will," said Ed.

"And who is first?" said laz.

"Me, I'm first," said Emily.

Amanda was surprised when Emily confidently spoke up.

It went into the records that Emily was first, Amanda second, Tadhg third, and gentlemanly Ed last. They were all mostly happy with that.

At least they had run a loop of the world's hardest race within the time limit. They were actually ten minutes under the time limit for one loop, but it would be impossible to continue. None of them wanted to run any more anyway. They were recorded as "DNF-ers" (Did Not Finishers). Laz pretended he didn't want to see their hard-earned book pages, but finally counted them.

Amanda felt humiliated when Danger Dave blew *Taps* on the bugle for her. They all stood silently as *Taps* was played once for each of them, indicating their race was done.

The two men walked down to the showers, but Amanda and Emily walked up to the campfire and sat in a couple of chairs to warm up and rest for a few minutes.

Emily spoke first. "That was fun. You know, if we get in next year, we should plan to run together again," she said.

Amanda rolled her eyes, and looked at Emily like she was an idiot.

"We did pretty well together, didn't we? Two is better than one, and if we stick together, we can conquer this thing and be the first women finishers," said Emily.

"I don't know. You're such a baby about dark tunnels," said Amanda.

"But I made it just fine, and it won't be a problem

anymore!" said a vehement Emily.

"O.K.," said a tired Amanda.

"O.K. you'll run with me? Or just O.K.?" asked Emily.

Laz was sneaking around behind them, listening to their conversation. He had a strange smile on his face.

"OK, I'll run with you. If we both get in," said a very reluctant Amanda.

"Shake on it," said Emily, sticking out her hand.

Amanda sighed and shook her hand, too tired to argue with Emily.

Behind them, laz was poking around the picnic table searching for something to eat, and quietly laughed his evil little laugh, "*Heh, heh, heh, heh...*"

"What do you think, Kate? Will a woman ever finish this race? He was asking RawDog's wife, an older, gray-haired woman who was sitting peacefully at the picnic table.

She looked up at laz with inquisitive eyes and said, "The jury is still out on that one. I guess we'll just have to wait and see, won't we?"

.

ATTEMPT TWO

Chapter 19: Whistle Up a Storm

She reflected about her family and how glad they would be to see her when she returned from this hell. They must be worried sick. Her husband might have left camp and come out looking for her already, knowing she had been away too long and might be lost and in a desperate predicament. She just had to find her way out of these woods. Too many people would be anxious and afraid for her.

The hiking poles were not going to be her ticket out of the ravine, but she made sure they were secured in the back of her pack so she could use them later. She left the water bottles and padding on the tops of the poles.

Crawling was the only solution. She would have to claw her way to the top. She knew she could travel downhill, the same direction the water was flowing through the area, but she feared it was too steep and rocky that way and she might fall again. She wanted to climb out of the little ravine and then follow the base of the rock wall southeast in hopes that it would meet the trail at the boundary of the park.

She pushed apart the coals of her little fire using a

stick, and used a rock to scrape up some dirt to smother the coals with. She pushed her remaining gear into the back of her pack, then reached into the front pocket of her pack to get her leather gloves. Her fingers came upon something small and hard. She pulled it out, and looked at it in wonder. It was her whistle. She had totally forgotten about her whistle!

She put it to her lips and blew as hard as she could. The shrill blast tore into her ears, and she quickly put her hands up to cover them, and kept blowing. Over and over she blew blasts of hot air through the whistle, creating wondrous noise in the quiet woodlands. If anyone was out there nearby, they would surely hear it. She waited after many blasts, listening, but there was no answering cry or noise of any kind except the ringing in her ears.

She put the whistle into the pocket, thinking she would try again later, huffing deeply with frustration. There was nothing left to do but pray. She whimpered out a prayer, asking for help from God above, but she knew that God helps those who help themselves, and she must crawl or die.

Chapter 20: Try Try Again

When Amanda arrived in Denver, Robbie picked her up at the airport and took her home. She was quiet and introspective, and he looked worried about her.

She unpacked and changed clothes, with Robbie exclaiming over the "rat bites" on her legs from all the briers, her scraped-up arms and back, her filthy, holey tights and shorts, and her blistered feet. He said, "I bet you're glad to be done with that!"

"It was rough. But I'm going to do it again. I need to finish it," she said stubbornly.

"Honey, if you couldn't do it this year, what makes you think you can do it next year?" Usually Amanda succeeded at everything she tried, and he was used to her coming home victorious.

"I will do it. You will see. I need to change my strategy is all," she said.

"Tell me what you will do differently," he said, remembering all her intense preparations.

Amanda had been seriously thinking about that all the way home on the airplane. Her second year she wanted to be ready to go it alone. It would be nice if she could follow a fast veteran of the race, but it was unlikely that would happen, unless someone asked her to run with them. She remembered Emily's request that they run it together, but she really didn't want to do that. She knew she had shook hands on it, and she couldn't get out of it. But maybe she could accidentally scrape Emily somewhere out there.

She told Robbie some of her ideas. "I think if a woman is to finish, she has to lead, she has to navigate, and she has to move fast and light. She has to leave her security zone."

She continued, "My plan is to learn the race route better, practice my navigation skills both during daylight hours and nighttime, learn how to navigate in the fog, spend time running in the rain and cold, do more training on vertical, and work on my speed."

"That's quite a list," he said, whistling.

"Yes, and during the actual race I will try to stay with the lead pack for at least the first two books, so I can build up a buffer of time to take naps in camp between loops."

"Sounds good. What else?" Robbie asked her.

"I need to have a crew to get me through camp and back into the race quickly after each loop. I really need you to be able to help me with that."

"All I can do is try. Maybe I can get off work then," responded Robbie. He obviously wanted to be there for her.

She had spent her time on the airplane home writing down her new strategy. She also made a list of all the landmarks she could remember, and any bits of information she had gleaned from Frozen Ed.

She also decided she would try to get into the fall mini-version of the race so that she had some more time under her belt out there. Also, if she managed to come in first in that race, she had immediate entry into the big race in the spring.

About once a month she received an email from Emily. Emily wanted to know what she had been doing for training, and how it was going. Amanda always replied, but never told her everything. This endeavor was hers alone, and she didn't really want to share it with another person.

She set about racing and winning some really hard races that year, to add weight to her entry. Because she had completed a loop, she already had a little weight in the entry drawing.

Her entry essay about why she should be allowed into the race would be stellar this time. She planned to write it in cryptogram form*, so Iaz would have to decipher it. She had heard that he liked puzzles, so this would be a doozy. That should give her more weight in the entry process. Writing her essay took up a whole hour, and she knew Iaz would be excited to receive it.

"B CBAA GW FRW HBSUF CENJK FE HBKBUR FRBU SJLW KE NJFFWS CRJF. XEP RJYW NX CESI EK FRJF. B JN KEF FEE UEHF!"

She even gave him the translation of a few of the letters: W=E, F=T, N=M, and S=R.

When the time came to learn if she had gained entry, she was thrilled to receive a condolence email, written in the same cryptogram code* she had used for her entry essay. It said:

"JAA CENWK JSW FEE UEHF!"

She could see that she and Iaz were likely to have some good arguments.

Right after she opened it and deciphered it, she received a text from Emily saying she was in, and was Amanda? Amanda replied with a simple, "Yes."

Emily sent a happy text saying, "We're both in! We're going to kill it!"

Amanda didn't feel that special bond that Emily thought they had achieved in the first race.

She wanted to be the first woman to finish the race, just her, and her alone.

Why should she share her glory?

ATTEMPT TWO

Chapter 21: Sassy

She made sure the fire was completely covered with dirt and there was no chance it could come back to life. Then she began to crawl up the slope, pushing off with her knees, and clawing through the muck with her leather-clad hands. She pulled and pushed up about ten feet, then heard a whimpering noise at the lip of the hill. She looked up, and saw a large form staring down.

It was barking a greeting. The dog was huge, and dark red, with long ears, and wrinkles descending its face to a mouth filled with slobber. The dog drooled and slung the spit left and right, as it lumbered down the slope towards her. She knew dogs, and this one was definitely friendly.

The dog came right to her and began licking her. The spit from its enormous mouth dripped all over her face.

She covered her face with one hand, and said, "Stop it! Wait! No, sit!"

The dog was confused, and began jumping about, joyful to have found a friend.

She sat up and said, "Okay, boy, er… girl, you've found me! Sit down now!"

The dog sat right next to her, and leaned into her, causing her to start falling down the hill again. She wrapped her arms around the dog's neck, and the two of them slid to the bottom. The dog sat still beside her, breathing hard, and still slobbering.

She grabbed the collar around its neck, and read the inscription on a brass plate out loud: "Sassy IV. Property of BMSP."

There was also a phone number engraved on the plate. Of course, if she had a phone, she would call the number and return the dog, but she did not. The dog was not leaving and seemed to want her to be its owner for the present time.

God had answered her prayer for help. She was sure of it. The dog had come to help her out of the ravine. She rubbed its massive head and strong shoulders, and thought about sled dogs. She knew her dog breeds, and this one was a ruby red bloodhound, but it could still pull her easily. If she could figure out the right commands, she could be free from this place of despair.

The dog had a long leather leash hanging from the

clip on its collar. It must have jerked it loose from its owner. She could hold onto it and get Sassy to drag her along the ground. It would hurt, but it was better than crawling.

She held onto the leash so the dog wouldn't take off, and used her other hand to pull the bivy sack out of the loops on the back of her pack. She had an idea that she could use it to aid in her escape, and she looked it over carefully. It was slick, and it might slide along the ground with her in it. If she wrapped up in all her clothes and rain gear, she might have enough padding to prevent too much pain. At least she could use it to get pulled out of the little ravine.

She put her pack on her back and climbed inside the bivy so she was lying on her stomach. It was a tight squeeze for her splinted foot. Her arms and head stuck out so she looked like a grub.

Holding the leash tightly in both hands, she yelled, "Okay Sassy, take off!"

Sassy sat there, watching her, and licked her nose.

"Sassy! Giddyap!"

Sassy totally ignored her then, and began chewing at her own hip, like there was an urgent itch.

What were the right words? How about something simpler. She hollered, "GO!"

Sassy jumped up and took off like a child released to recess. She climbed up the hill easily, dragging her new friend behind. Sassy didn't struggle with the weight behind her at all. She appeared to be experienced at having a cargo to pull.

Suddenly they were at the top, and Sassy's sidekick was ecstatic to be out of the ravine. "Yes!" she screamed. She was free!

The way after that was rough and rocky. She worried that the bivy sack wouldn't make it. She would have to use her makeshift crutches from here on out. She checked her map again. She planned to spend more time on the ridgeline than in the rock-filled creek beds.

She used her hiking pole crutches as much as she could, falling often, but hauling herself back up over and over. Sometimes she crawled hand over hand, pulling herself forward inches at a time over the roughest terrain. Sometimes she had to maneuver her body over and under obstacles like downed trees. She kept bashing her injured ankle, so she decided it needed more protection. She wrapped the bivy sack around her ankle over and over until it was mummified, then wrapped the remaining duct tape around it. She wasn't able to hold Sassy's leash, but Sassy stayed nearby anyway, watching and waiting to be needed again. The dog had adopted her.

It was a long, tedious, painful journey, and she wondered if she would ever make it out.

ATTEMPT TWO

Chapter 22: Scraping Miss Emily

Their second year's race began with Amanda trying to push to the front of the pack again. She figured Emily was right behind her, but she didn't bother looking back. The race had started in the early morning darkness, and she had not noticed Emily as the runners crowded around the gate. There were several people ahead of Amanda in the long line of competitors speeding up the first mountain. Their high-powered headlamps lit up the trail before them.

Amanda planned to stay with the lead pack at least through Book 2, if she could keep up. She arrived at Book 1 and tore out her page, then followed the pack down the difficult Jaquemate Hill. This time she had improved her leg speed on descents, and managed to almost stay with them. She was climbing down through a patch of thick briers, when she saw Emily waiting for her below. How had Emily gotten ahead of her?

"What are you doing down there? I thought you were behind me?" she said, incredulous.

Emily said she had hurried to Book 1 ahead of the pack and torn out her page first. Then she had not seen Amanda and decided to wait for her.

Amanda couldn't believe it. Emily had gotten to Book 1 first? She must not have seen her in the darkness. How could she have become that fast in only a year? And she had actually found Book 1 all by herself? Her opinion of Emily might need some ratcheting up.

Amanda led from then on, with Emily not too far behind. Amanda had to push herself extra hard to stay ahead. Sometimes Emily caught up and they conferred about navigation or finding books, but mostly Amanda hurried to books, tore out her page, and left before Emily arrived, so Emily had to figure things out on her own. Amanda reasoned that Emily needed the experience.

Sometimes when Emily caught up, she asked Amanda to wait for her, and for them to do it together, but Amanda just shrugged and said, "Keep up and we will." She wanted badly to run her own race.

She hoped Emily would finally give up on this togetherness thing, and fall behind or get off course.

But Emily wouldn't disappear. She hung on for dear life, always just seconds behind, and mostly in sight.

They both were barely surviving when they started the counterclockwise fourth loop. Loop Four was virgin territory for both of them. Robbie had been doing a good job getting Amanda set up and out of camp quickly, and she had managed to take a nap or two. Emily's husband and children had come and were taking care of her.

Not many people were still in the race, but they had both seen Danger Dave a few times. It looked like he was going to make his first Fun Run of three loops this year. Sam was ahead of them, and probably completing his fourth loop and returning to the course for his fifth. Amanda wondered if he would choose clockwise or counterclockwise for his fifth loop, as the runner in first was allowed to choose the direction for his or her final loop.

She believed clockwise would be easier because the imprint from the first loop would be the strongest, and that is the direction she would choose if she ever made it to the final loop and had a choice.

She made it to Book 3 on the fourth loop. Emily was right behind her, yelling her name. She pushed on ahead anyway, ignoring the calls. She didn't see her later on when she left Book 2.

The fog was rolling in when she left the creek and began ascending Jaquemate Hill. She climbed up the Flume of Doom with no problems. She reached

Book 1, and found the book still lying where she had left it earlier, on top of the heavy rock, still zipped up in its plastic bag. She noticed the title of the book for the first time: *You'll Never Catch Me!* Amanda thought the title was a strange coincidence.

Her unwanted sidekick was nowhere in sight. She continued on to the candyass trail into camp to victoriously finish Loop Four.

ATTEMPT TWO

Chapter 23: The River

Sassy was still trotting along ahead of her most of the way, with a few totally necessary side trips chasing after chipmunks. It was a relief to have her company on this arduous journey.

When she came to a trail, she was pretty sure where they were, but she pulled out her map and compass. She thought they were near the park's boundary heading south, pretty close to the corner of the park. She could see a faint trail next to the creek on her map. She hoped she was approaching that. It might be the way out of the mountains and home to civilization. She had heard that there was a road over there that the locals use for hunting. Otherwise, she would have to climb up the steep trail to the top of the mountain, then down the switchbacks into the campground. Normally she could run that in less than an hour, but not today. She had a gut feeling that a road was nearby.

She pulled out her whistle and blew on it some more, covering her ears. Still, no one came to save her. But Sassy was madly jumping around, driven half-crazy by the whistles. Her mistress pulled off her bloody buff and left it there on the trail, in case someone came by looking for her.

Her elbows and arms were beaten up from crawling, and her leather-gloved hands were sore from clutching the hiking poles. The hand with the bite wound was particularly troublesome. She was bound to have a bad case of poison ivy on her face from being so close to the ground, and she wondered how bad the ticks were this spring. She had protected her broken ankle as best she could by padding it and holding it up. The rest of her body had taken a beating, and she felt like someone's punching bag.

"Let's go," she said to Sassy, putting away her whistle, map and compass.

She hopped past the cairn at the corner of the park, and made her way slowly through a rocky creek bed, desperately trying not to fall any more. Then she had to crawl up into the woods on her elbows and knees. The makeshift crutches did not do well on up-hills. Soon she could see the trail widening, and it changed into large, lumpy gravel which she was able to hop through on her crutches. Suddenly, Sassy came to a stop at the bank of a small river. The bloodhound whined, unsure what to do.

Now what? She thought she was almost out of the

woods, and another obstacle was being thrown at her. She didn't want to crawl through the river, and worried the current would knock her down on her crutches. She didn't know what to do next. She pulled out her whistle and blew on it some more, making long cries of anguish resound throughout the forest. Sassy howled at the sky with each blast, then suddenly took off into the forest after a squirrel.

She sat there at the edge of the river feeling sorry for herself. She had come so far, and now she was stymied and alone. She pulled out the peanut butter and jelly sandwich she had been hoarding, and gobbled it up.

She peered ahead, and wondered if the way out was close by. If she could manage to cross the river, she might find the road not too far away. Then she would have to hobble down that road until she found civilization, or wait where she was for a car or a rescue crew to come get her.

She was still in the stubborn mind-set of self-extraction. Laz had said that help was not coming. There had never been need for a search and rescue operation at any of the races over the years. She didn't intend for there to be one for her.

She drank some of her water. Then she took a

moment to blow her whistle again. She prepared to use her hiking poles to get across the river. As she was standing up, using the poles to lean on, she heard someone coming from the trail behind her. She looked back, and there was a small, determined figure running frantically towards her.

They saw each other at the same moment. She heard her name being screamed.

"Emily!"

ATTEMPT TWO

Chapter 24: Back in Camp

Everyone was waiting at the Yellow Gate. The crowd of people were yelling her name.

"Amanda! Go Amanda!"

When she touched the gate, they milled around her and patted her on the back, saying, "Great job!" and "Good work!" Everyone was so proud of her for being the first woman to ever finish a fourth loop.

She was exhausted and needed to sleep again before she left on her final loop. She gave laz her book pages for the count. Robbie was there, and together they hurried down to their campsite so she could eat and get some well-deserved rest.

Amanda knew she had to get some sleep before she could return to the race. She changed her clothes, then lay down and said, "Wake me in two hours, please."

She slept fitfully, thrashing and worrying about Emily. She had a bad intuition that something was wrong. Finally, Robbie shook her shoulder and told her she had twenty minutes to leave camp.

Robbie had already prepared her food and liquids,

so she focused on stuffing her mouth with scrambled eggs and banana, drinking as much chocolate almond milk as she could in between bites. She put on fresh socks and shoes, then she slung her pack on her back, and they hurried to the gate.

A sleepy looking young boy with disheveled, blonde hair suddenly ran up to her and asked, "Have you seen my Mom? She was with you when you started on Loop Four."

It was Emily's oldest son, Michael. He must have been sleeping, and woke up to check on his Mom.

Emily's husband, Rick, hurried up to her as well, with fear and worry written all over his face. "What happened to my wife?" he asked.

Shame washed over her and she could not answer them right away. She had left Emily behind. Her pride and yearning for glory had caused her to be a mean and selfish person. Finally, she said, "I don't know. I haven't seen her in a while."

"But she said she was going to stay with you through the whole race. That you two had shook hands on it. She was so confident that you could do it together," said her worried husband.

"The race is so hard, and you never know what is

going to happen out there. I don't know where she is. She was right behind me most of the way, and then she wasn't. I had to keep moving."

Rick asked laz if Emily had made it back yet, but he said no. Michael rushed up to the Yellow Gate and grabbed laz by the arm. "I'm going out there. My Mom needs me! I have to find her!"

Laz was shocked at the young boy's outburst, but quickly recovered, and said, "No, you can't go out there. She'll make it back soon. It will be okay."

The boy began pacing behind the gate, and his father came up to comfort and restrain him. "Will you send out a search party?" he asked laz.

"We have a record of 100% self-extraction at this race. She should return on her own. They always turn up eventually," said laz. He didn't think Emily had been away long enough for anyone to be worried.

Amanda was watching this scene, horrified at what she had done. She hung her head and turned away. Her husband asked her what was wrong.

"I left her," whispered Amanda. "I just wanted to win," she confided.

Robbie looked at her in surprise. "But you shook on it," he said.

"I know. She was always right behind me, but it was annoying, and I scraped her at Book 3." She felt so ashamed.

"So she must be close behind you. Did you see her at Book 2 or Book 1?"

"Noooooo," she moaned. "I just kept going."

"She'll turn up. She's probably messed up a bearing and gotten off course. She'll figure it out."

Laz had become somewhat concerned, and said, "We're sending Ralph up ahead of you to check Book 1 for Emily's page. If it's still there, we may have to send out a search party later today."

"If anything happens to Emily, it is all my fault," Amanda whispered to Robbie, feeling morose.

"She'll be okay," said Robbie, hugging her.

She looked up at him, and their gaze held briefly. Suddenly, she made up her mind. She got that strong, determined set to her jaw. Robbie instinctively knew what she was going to do.

Ralph was standing next to laz, ready to run. Amanda touched the gate, and Ralph took off running ahead of her. She didn't have the choice of which way to go on her fifth loop, as Sam had already begun his fifth loop going counterclockwise. She was glad to get the clockwise direction, though, and left the gate at a fast paced hike.

"Good luck!" yelled Robbie to her back.

The two hour nap had helped her immensely, and the food and liquids. But she could never catch Ralph, as he had fresh legs.

She left on her fifth loop in the clockwise direction, hoping desperately that she would come across Emily. The cowbell clanged morosely behind her, telling everyone in camp that she was on her final loop.

But she had no intention of running a final loop.

ATTEMPT TWO

Chapter 25: Amanda to the Rescue

Amanda was grateful Sam had taken the counterclockwise direction, because otherwise she would have been out in the woods for hours before she entered the vicinity where Emily was probably lost. As she was running down through the Deep Woods, Ralph came trotting towards her. He had already been to Book 1 and was on his way back to camp.

"Did you find her page?" asked Amanda.

"Yes, it's still there!" replied Ralph, striding right by her and continuing up through the forest. "Good luck!" he hollered back.

Amanda's brain was full of a hundred worries. *What if Emily had been lost all night? What if she had gotten hurt? What if she was finding her way to camp by a different route? What if a wild animal had attacked her? What if they never found her?*

She continued on to Book 1, then down Jaquemate Hill, looking everywhere for signs of Emily. She didn't see any sign of her anywhere, so she continued on the boundary trail to the ridgeline, then down to Book 2 at the confluence. There was still no sign of Emily, but her page was missing, so she knew she had been there. That meant Emily was lost or injured somewhere in between Book 2 and Book 1. That was some nasty territory, with steep, brier-covered mountains and cliffs. She took a short break to eat and drink, becoming increasingly anxious with every moment. Amanda had a bad feeling deep inside that something awful had happened to Emily. She headed back the way she had come, up to the boundary trail on the ridge.

When she got to the corner of the park, she found a brightly colored buff lying on the trail. It looked like the one Emily had been wearing, but it was covered with dried blood, causing Amanda's heart to beat faster. She decided to take a chance and head out to the old back road that Frozen Ed had told them about. Surely Emily would remember about that, and travel that way if she needed rescue.

It crossed her mind briefly that she was travelling off-course, and the glory of finishing the race was slipping right through her fingers. She had a fleeting moment of regret, but continued on.

She heard a shrill, high-pitched sound in the distance, and hurried down the trail until she could hear it better. Yes, it was a whistle! It must be Emily using her emergency whistle. She also heard a dog howling miserably.

She ran as hard as she could towards the sounds, and then she saw her! Emily was standing at an odd angle, leaning on her two hiking poles, with one leg held up behind her.

"Emily!" she yelled, in happy recognition.

She ran to her, and Emily lifted her arms in greeting, causing her homemade crutches to fall away from her. She burst into tears when Amanda grabbed her up in a hug.

Amanda was crying too. "What happened? Where were you? I'm so sorry!" Amanda was talking all in a rush of breath.

Emily wiped tears out of her eyes, and stood there on one leg, gazing at Amanda with love in her eyes. Amanda couldn't take it, and tore her gaze away, ashamed.

"I got kind of lost, and fell off the cliff into a little ravine. I couldn't get out with a broken ankle, but I tried so hard, over and over all night. How is my family? My children? Have you seen them?"

Amanda told her about her son wanting to come out looking for her. Emily beamed with pride.

Amanda bent down and picked up the crutches and gave them to Emily. "So is it broken or just sprained?"

"I'm pretty sure it's broken. It hurts terribly to put weight on it, and I heard it crack," replied Emily.

Emily tucked the crutches under her arms. "I have used these a lot, but sometimes I had to crawl," she said. "And a dog came and helped me. She pulled me out of the ravine. Oh, there she is! Sassy!"

Sassy came running from the woods towards them, wagging her tail with joy. She stopped in front of Emily and sat down, swishing her tail in the dirt and looking up adoringly. Emily stroked her massive head.

Amanda didn't much like dogs, but reached out tentatively to pet her. Sassy sniffed her hand and let her pet her head.

"You crawled and hopped on one leg through that horrible territory? That's impossible!"

Emily responded in a thoughtful voice, "I've always believed that if you have faith and are motivated, nothing is impossible."

Amanda's eyes widened, and she sighed. "I guess so. Just like this race. It's totally impossible for anyone to ever finish five loops out here. But somehow a few people do manage to finish it."

"They're motivated," said Emily, nodding her head in agreement. Inwardly, she reflected upon her own motivation, beginning with the small flame of desire to do the race and then the raging fire inside herself to get off the mountain and away from the Bad Thing.

Emily looked fondly at Sassy. "Sassy seems to have had some experience pulling weight behind her. She pulled me right out of that ravine after I had tried to crawl out all night. I used my bivy sack to get inside and be dragged along behind her."

Amanda noticed that the bivy sack was now wrapped around Emily's injured ankle.

Amanda looked at Emily with grudging respect. "I guess you took care of yourself," she said.

"No, I couldn't get out of there. But God sent me Sassy, and she pulled me out," she said, affectionately rubbing Sassy's ears.

Amanda thought it had all been pure, blind luck. She changed the subject and said, "We could camp here and wait, or cross the river and start walking on the old road towards town."

"We'll be more likely to be found if we make it to the road," said Emily. "But I couldn't figure out how to cross the river."

"I can help you across the river," said Amanda. "Here, lean on me and we can do it together."

Amanda put her hand in her pocket and said, "Oh, here, I found this. Good clue you left." She handed Emily her buff.

Emily slid the buff gently over her injured head, letting it hang in a loop around her neck. She stuffed her poles into the back of her pack and shouldered it again.

They looked at the swiftly flowing water of the dark green river. It was about twenty feet or more across. It would be slippery and cold.

Emily put her arm around Amanda's shoulders and leaned on her as they hobbled across the river together. Amanda was so much shorter that her shoulders were the right height for Emily's arm. Amanda wrapped her arm around Emily's waist to steady her. The water was almost knee level from yesterday's rain, and the bottom was slick with algae.

Amanda walked slowly across, helping Emily maneuver through the slippery rocks, warning, "Be careful, it's bad here."

Emily hopped on her healthy foot, and Amanda kept her from falling a time or two. They made it safely to the other bank, and sat down briefly.

Emily was concerned about Amanda abandoning

her fifth loop and her chance at being the first woman to finish the race.

Amanda shrugged it off and said, "Oh well. There's always next year."

They were quiet for a minute, then Emily had a question. "Do you remember the story Tadhg told us about the Bad Thing?"

"Yes, but it *was* just a story," said Amanda firmly.

"No, no, it wasn't JUST a story. It was true! It came and attacked me last night!" She proceeded to tell Amanda about the attack and how she had killed the creature, but it came back to life.

She bent down and stretched out her buff to show her the wounds on the back of her head and neck. Amanda stared in wonder. Although she could see the wounds before her eyes, there was no way she could believe an immortal creature existed and inflicted those wounds. There must be some other explanation.

She thought about it for a minute, and remembered something she had read on the Internet recently. She told Emily that she was certain that her Bad Thing was merely a Great Horned Owl. She had read about them attacking if someone entered their nesting territory. They were fierce protectors of their young. Emily must have been below a nest.

Emily could not accept this simple explanation, and said that Amanda didn't know what she was talking about. "You weren't even there! It most definitely was not an owl! Owls are not that big and heavy, and don't have such an enormous wingspan! Besides, I'd know an owl if I saw one!"

Amanda told her that the Great Horned Owl can have a six foot wingspan at full growth. Also her fear of the Bad Thing made it appear bigger and heavier than it really was.

"And your 4th loop exhaustion must have caused you to be practically hallucinating," Amanda said. "The stress of falling off the cliff and breaking your ankle was also part of it. Your mind was confused and imagined the Bad Thing out of an owl!"

Emily shook her head back and forth. "You weren't there! How could you know?"

Amanda shrugged angrily and said, "Believe what you want, but you're wrong."

They stood up stiffly and made their way from the river bank to an open yellow gate. "This looks like the Yellow Gate in camp, but that one is never open," said Emily, somewhat puzzled.

There was a gravel road beyond the gate, but no

traffic at all. "This must be the old backwoods road that hunters use," said Amanda. "Frozen Ed told us that if you turn left, you will eventually get to town. Go right, and you travel deeper into the backcountry."

It was an easy choice. They began hobbling down the road towards civilization.

"Listen, I'm sorry I left you behind," Amanda suddenly spilled out. "I was selfish and mean. I wanted to be the first woman to finish. I'm so sorry you got lost and hurt!"

"It's okay, I understand. It was my own fault. I never should have made you shake on staying together. This race is not a team race. You have to be able to do it on your own. Don't worry about it anymore," said Emily graciously, and kissed Amanda on top of her head.

Amanda was surprised by Emily's understanding and forgiveness. The sweetness of the moment enveloped her and lifted the worries from her soul. She felt like she was walking on air, holding onto her new friend's waist as they slowly made their way down the road.

ATTEMPT TWO

Chapter 26: Bubba and Bud Take the Wheel

"I'm worried I will never run again," said Emily.

"Sure you will. The hospital will fix you up, and you'll be training again in no time," said Amanda.

"Do you really think so?" asked Emily.

"Yes, absolutely. You've got the determination and drive it takes to do something like this. Look at how you got yourself out of that fix you were in, and you're still going."

"I really wanted to do it this year. I was anxious to find my limits and learn about my endurance. I think I found out more than I wanted to know. Do you still want to finish it, Amanda?"

"Yes, of course! Next year, if he lets me in again."

"I doubt I can do it by then," said Emily sadly.

"Then maybe two years out. Just don't give up. It's a crazy goal, but you have to keep trying for what you want to do," said Amanda with conviction.

As they continued making progress down the rutted roadway, they began to hear loud popping noises from somewhere off in the distance behind them.

"Gunshots," said Emily.

"Hunters?" asked Amanda.

"No, I don't think so. It's not hunting season, and those sound like they are coming from a revolver," replied Emily.

"How do you know that?" asked Amanda.

"I've been around guns my whole life. Grew up shooting cans in the back yard. Used to go coon hunting with my cousins."

The gunshots were getting closer. Amanda was feeling really nervous and shaky.

All of a sudden, the gunshots were much louder.

"Here, let's get into the trees and hide somewhere," said Amanda.

"No, let's wait and see," disagreed Emily. "It's probably local boys out joy-riding."

Soon an ancient, beat up, green pickup truck was approaching them from behind. They could see two men in the cab, and one was still shooting out the window at something and hollering, "*Whoo!* Hot dang!"

The driver saw them and started honking the horn: *whooga!*

The truck rushed at them, then stopped in a smothering cloud of exhaust smoke.

"Well, if it ain't Sassy!" yelled one of the men out the window.

"Oh, you in a heap o' trouble now!" hollered the other one.

"Gonna have to take you back to prison. You gonna be punished!" said the first one, in a sing-song, whiny voice.

The two young women huddled together and Sassy leaned against Emily, trembling.

The two men clambered out of the truck with great difficulty. The young women could see that they were a pair of old geezers with faces as drawn down with wrinkles as Sassy's was. Their skulls were swathed in fuzzy hair, with long beards and equally long white hair. They apparently ate well, as their stomachs bulged out over the tops of their jeans.

Too many pies and cakes and corn muffins, Amanda thought to herself, staring at them.

They stomped up to Amanda and Emily, and stood in front of them, ogling them up and down with old, faded eyes behind thick-lensed glasses. The two of them looked like twins, but it could be just the uniform of old age that makes every old man look alike.

"Well, now, what have we here?" said the driver, hiking up his drawers with both hands and sucking in his breath.

"Looks like two lost little girls!" said the other fellow in a flirty tone.

Amanda started to speak, but Emily poked her and whispered, "Let me handle this."

"We've been out in the woods all night running that race in the park," she said sweetly. "We really need some help. Do you two nice fellers think you could give us a ride into town?"

Amanda could have sworn that Emily's voice suddenly changed into a sweet and sticky country drawl.

The two old men looked taken aback. One of them said, "You're in that thar famous race? That hunnert mile race through all them briers back thar? The one they made that movie about? You don't say!"

"Well, I'll be hornswoggled!" said the other one.

"Yes, I was out all last night, lost in the woods. And

112

I fell off a cliff and broke my ankle. It hurts so much," she said in her best girlish voice, lifting her ankle higher so they could see.

"You young girls was really in that race? A hunnert miles up and down these hills and hollers?" the driver asked in disbelief.

"Yes, we made it nearly 80 miles when this happened. We are so tired and thirsty," said Emily woefully.

"Well, now, we can give you a lift, for sartin," said one. "Listen up, I'm forgettin' my manners," he said, removing his cap. "I'm Bubba Hicks, and this here is my brother, Bud. We used to be guards at the old prison back in the day. We do everything together; why, we even married sisters. We've both got the pro-strate cancer, too," he said, gazing at them solemnly. "About all we can do now is drive around back in here and shoot at varmints, but it's a life."

"So how'd you come by little Miss Houdini, thar?" asked Bud, nodding towards Sassy.

Emily told how Sassy had pulled her out of the ravine, petting her head while she talked. Sassy had settled down and stopped trembling, but she still didn't approach the Hicks brothers.

"That figgers. Some of the guards at the prison use the dogs for hauling out the deer they shoot," said Bud.

"That Sassy! Ain't she somethin'!" Bubba whistled appreciatively. "You know her great grandma was the one to track down ol' James Earl Ray. She comes from a long line of good hunters."

Bubba looked down and shuffled his feet. "Dogs don't like us much. We used to be mean ol' codgers, and they can sense that. But we is reformed now! Honest to goodness! We wouldn't lay a hand on a dog, or a foot neither."

"Cause we cain't hardly get about, much less kick or hit," snickered Bud.

"We oughter get these girls into the back of the truck now," said Bubba to Bud.

"Heard dat!" said Bud in response.

Bubba pulled down the tail gate, and then had to shuffle things around in the bed of the truck for a few minutes. "Here, let's get these boards over those holes," he said to Bud.

"Heard dat!" said Bud again.

The two of them managed to cover up the rusted out holes in the bed with some old boards to make places for Amanda and Emily to sit. They tried to help them crawl into the back of the truck, but they didn't need much help. Emily sat on the tail gate and swung her good leg up into the truck, then pulled up the bad leg. Then she scooted onto a board with her back against the side of the bed. Amanda couldn't reach the tail gate to sit on it, and Bubba showed her how to put her foot up on the bumper and pull herself in. She sat across from Emily. Next, they had to get Sassy to jump in, but Sassy was still afraid to come near them. Emily called her, and Sassy finally took a running jump into the bed of the truck, practically landing in Emily's lap.

"There, there, you did it!" said Emily, rubbing Sassy's side.

The two old geezers squeezed their girths into the cab, and Bubba tried to turn over the engine. It whined and shook, but did not start. "Dag nab it!" he muttered.

"You got to fiddle with that loose wire, ya think? Or does it need some earl?" asked Bud.

"Dunno. Have to go check," said Bubba, pouring himself slowly out of the cab. He lifted up the hood of the truck and peered inside.

Bud pointed at the cooler in the bed through the

broken out rear window. He said, "Hep yerselves to a Bud, girls."

Amanda shook her head no, remembering the effects of the Irish whiskey on the Zipline, but Emily was thirsty. "I'm almost out of water," she said apologetically to Amanda, as she reached in and grabbed a cold one. There were only three left, and she offered one to Bud.

He took it happily, and asked for the other one for Bubba. She gave him that one as well. "For after he gets the truck fixed," he said.

They popped open their cans and took big swigs. Bud said, "Whar you girls from, anyhow?"

"Denver," said Amanda.

"Whoowheee! That's a fur piece," said Bud.

"I'm from across the ridge, Briceville," said Emily.

"Huh! A local girl! You hear that, Bubba? We got a local girl runnin' that race!"

Bubba looked out from under the hood, smiled, and said, "Heard dat!"

Pretty soon Bubba lowered the hood, wiped his greasy hands on a rag hanging out of his back pocket, and pushed his body back behind the steering wheel. He got the engine to turn over the first try, and Bud handed him his celebratory beer. He popped the top and took a long swallow, and burped. Bud belched in response. They both laughed. The truck started chugging down the road with a lurch. The two young women held on to the sides of the truck, and Sassy nearly fell. Emily told her to sit, so she did.

They were winding their way along the jeep road, bumping through the ruts, when Bud suddenly pulled out his revolver and squeezed off a round or two out the window.

Sassy's ears twitched, but she did not jump out of the truck.

"What are you shooting at?" asked Amanda, shook up and surprised.

"Oh, any ol' thing that moves. Varmints, ya know. Mostly coyotes," said Bud through the glass-less rear window. He threw his empty can out the cab window into the ditch.

"But, but… you can recycle those," stuttered Amanda.

"Re-cycle? She wants us to re-cycle!" said Bud to Bubba.

"Heard dat!" wheezed Bubba, and kept driving.

"Do you really kill little animals?" asked Amanda.

"Nah, he cain't aim to save his own life!" said Bubba.

"Can too!" said Bud.

"Your eyesight ain't worth a dang!" said Bubba.

"Is too!" said Bud. "Why, I can hit a rabbit between its ears at forty paces!"

"Like to see that!" said Bubba.

"Just stop the truck and I'll show you!" said Bud.

"Nah, we got to do first things first!" said Bubba importantly.

They kept rolling. Amanda and Emily were bumping around in the bed, and Sassy almost jumped out a time or two, but they finally made it to the main highway.

Bubba pulled right into the oncoming traffic without stopping, then suddenly veered hard into the Quick Stop's parking lot.

Bubba left the engine running and hauled himself out of the cab. "Got to get some more beer," he said.

"Yeah, first things first!" yelled Bud.

"I reckon!" said Bubba, lumbering into the store, pulling at his pants pocket to get out his money.

Bud turned around a bit in the cab, and looked through the rear window. He said, "You girls run into the Bad Thing out thar?"

Emily was taken aback. She looked strangely at Amanda, then she spoke, "Yes, I did. It attacked me, but I killed it. Then it came back to life."

Amanda rolled her eyes. "There's no such thing as a Bad Thing!"

"Sure enough. That Bad Thing has been hangin' around in them thar woods for nigh on a hunnert years. Me and Bubba went out a few years back and tried to kill it. We spotted it up in the trees, and shot at it with our shotguns. Thought we had hit it a million times. Couldn't find the body, though. It's a haint, you know," he said, conspiratorially.

"A haint?" asked Amanda? "What's that?"

"The living dead. You know, like that TV show with the dead people running around eating the live people. It just won't die. Folks have been trying to kill it for ages round these parts," said Bud.

"It's an owl," said Amanda, flatly.

Bud started whooping and hollering and slapping

his knee. Bubba had made it back and was sticking the case of Budweiser into the cooler. Bud said, "She thinks the Bad Thing is just an owl!"

"An owl? Ha!" said Bubba. "You don't know nothin'! Now, the Bad Thing mates with the local owls sometimes, and they have strange, ugly babies. We shoot them every time we see them."

"But he's not an owl," said Bud.

"Okay, whatever," said Amanda, tired of this line of reasoning.

"I believe you," said Emily. "I saw it. It tried to haul me up into its nest."

"And you lived to tell about it? Girl, you is somethin' special!" said Bud.

Bubba pulled out two cans and shook one up and handed it to Bud through the cab's back window, grinning evilly.

Bud took it, and said, "Gall, dang it, Bubba, why'd you have to shake it?" Bud opened his door and popped the tab open outside the truck, foam spilling over the top of the can onto the asphalt.

Bubba asked the girls if they wanted one, but both declined this time.

"Okay, then, let's get this rescue oper-a-shun back in gear!" said Bubba, climbing in and getting settled. He pushed in the clutch with his left foot, put the truck into gear, eased off the clutch and floored the gas pedal. Away they went. He drove straight into the traffic without looking, and the truck jerked and rumbled to the state park turn off.

On the way, Bubba and Bud quaffed their beers quickly but did not throw the cans out this time. They did no more shooting either. Bud had put his revolver under the front seat, where his 22 rifle and shotgun lay.

They drove down the long road by the new prison, with Bud hanging out the window and hooting at the prisoners walking about the yard.

Bubba said, "Stop that! They cain't hear you!"

So Bud hooted and whistled louder.

They passed through the park entrance and by the Visitor Center. A ranger was pulling out in his vehicle, and Bud and Bubba both waved out the windows at him.

"Ranger Mike. Good guy," said Bubba.

They roared up the drive into the campground, neglecting to follow the arrows and drive around the bathhouse loop. Instead, they gunned it straight up to the Yellow Gate. Of course, the gate no longer stood in its original spot, so they had to keep going on up the road to stop at the new gate almost to the creek crossing.

Bubba turned off the engine and slowly climbed out of the cab. Some bystanders were watching them curiously. Bud managed to get out first and made it around to the rear of the truck, lowered the tailgate, and gave Amanda a hand to get down. Sassy leaped out and shook herself off, tongue lolling out as she surveyed the territory.

Emily's family came running up to the truck and surrounded the back end. "Mommy!" the kids were shouting and jumping up and down.

Laz came over and said, "Well, you made it back. I figured you would. We were just working on sending out the rescue squad to look for you."

Laz's dog, Little, normally so loveable and friendly, was going crazy with the presence of another dog in her territory, and wouldn't stop barking. Laz was scolding her repeatedly, "Little, stop it!" Finally, he had to grab her by the collar and haul her to the van for temporary imprisonment.

Emily's husband lifted her out of the truck and would not put her down. He held onto her for dear life, kissing her over and over.

Robbie was there too, and he grabbed Amanda up in a giant hug. "I knew you'd find her!" he said.

Bubba and Bud took their caps off, and stood there talking to laz and RawDog for a while, explaining how they found the girls and brought them to camp. They were quite proud of themselves. Someone took their picture by the Yellow Gate, and took down their address to send it to them. A newspaper reporter was there and took more pictures of all of them and wrote furiously in a spiral bound notebook.

"We've got to get you to the hospital!" said Emily's husband. He left her sitting in a lawn chair and ran down to get their van. When he returned, she hugged Sassy good bye, then Rick started to lift her into the van.

Laz interrupted them, saying, "Hold on a minute now. We've got to play *Taps*."

Danger Dave had finished his Fun Run earlier, and stood at the gate ready to play the bugle. Amanda stood before the gate with her hand over her heart as Danger blew the mournful tune for her. Then Rick stood holding Emily in his arms as Danger played it again for her. She burst into tears, then quickly wiped them away.

Finally, Rick lifted Emily into the van's front seat.

The children jumped in the sliding door. "I guess we'll come back later to get all our gear," Rick told RawDog.

Emily looked out the window and said, "How about you? Are you coming, Amanda?"

Amanda and Robbie climbed into the back of the van with all the children, and they turned around in a campsite driveway and were ready to go to the hospital.

But not before Bud came up to the open window of the van to give them some parting advice. Bud leaned on the window sill and gazed at Emily sitting in the passenger seat. "Now, remember, don't go out at night no more!"

"I won't. Thank you for stopping to help us," said Emily, smiling. "Please take good care of Sassy."

They took off for town, and Bubba and Bud kept on shooting the breeze with RawDog and laz for a while. Sassy was tied to a tree, waiting to go home.

Finally, they hauled themselves into their old, green truck. Someone untied Sassy and told her to jump up into the bed of the truck.

"Come on, Sassy! Let's take you back to prison!" yelled Bubba.

She leaped into the back end and lay down, resigned to her fate. Bubba cranked the starter and shoved the gear shift into reverse. The truck jerked into life again and poured out raw carbon monoxide smoke into the crowd of coughing onlookers. He backed it up, hanging his arm out the window and craning his neck to peer behind him. The side rearview mirror had ripped off long ago.

When they got to the campground loop, Bubba crunched it into first gear, and they took off downhill with a shudder and a roar. The Hicks brothers waved out the windows like celebrities, with Bud hooting and hollering all the way out of the campground.

Chapter 27: Trials and Terrors

Emily had no idea what to expect next, having never broken a bone before. She thought it was going to be an ordeal, though, but how could it be any worse than what she had already been through? She was wrong, of course, because she found out that going through surgery for a broken leg and then the resulting physical therapy were no walk in the park.

"What happened to you?" asked the doctor on duty, unwrapping her ankle and poking around on it.

"Ouch!" she yelped. "I took a little tumble."

"Looks like more than that. Did you hit anybody on the way down?"

She thought doctors always tried to be funny when they were making you hurt worse.

"Have you had anything to eat or drink in the last 12 hours?" He looked concerned.

"Yes, I did eat a peanut butter and jelly sandwich this morning, and I had a beer this afternoon," she admitted.

"Oh no. Well! So much for surgery today. We'll put you in first thing in the morning. Tonight you will have to spend here in the hospital."

Her husband later scoffed at that rule and told her, "Most likely he had a golf game this afternoon."

She was still in her filthy running clothes and her rain parka and pants. Unless Rick rushed back to camp and brought her some clean clothes, she was stuck wearing the dirty ones. She opted for the revealing hospital gown, though, to save him the trouble of the extra driving with the kids.

The nurses spent a lot of time cleaning up her leg, then focused on her other wounds from falling and from crawling through the woods. There were a lot of cuts, abrasions, and contusions to deal with, plus the talon puncture wounds at the base of her skull and the bite on her hand. She had to have some shots, too. This kept them busy for a while. Then they bandaged her up and put her in a room overnight.

Her family returned to the park to pack up all the camping gear, and then went home to get some rest. Amanda got some doctoring too, for her cuts and the blisters on her feet, then she and Robbie returned to camp with Emily's family to pack up their things.

All night, Emily tossed fitfully in the hospital bed, trying to sleep, but having dreams about the fall, the tortures of the race, and the Bad Thing.

"No, no, Stop it!" she screamed.

The male nurse on duty ran into her room to see what was wrong. "Do you want a sedative?"

She turned him down. Then, when she finally fell asleep from exhaustion, the nurse woke her up.

"Do you need anything to help you sleep?" he asked.

"You're kidding, right?" she asked, groggily.

"No, your doctor wants to make sure you are comfortable."

It was completely unbelievable the logic they had in hospitals. She told the nurse that she didn't need any pills except more acetaminophen. The nurse appeared disappointed, and made notes on the chart in his hands, then gave her the two acetaminophen she asked for.

She didn't like pain medication, and refused to take any. Only acetaminophen for her. Her mother had been addicted to pain meds after the car wreck that had killed Emily's father, and high as a kite most of the time, and that wasn't going to happen to her. The emotional suffering Emily had experienced after that trauma was worse than what she had just been through.

The surgery itself went smoothly to repair both her tibia and fibula, but recovery immediately afterwards was another nightmare. The pain was horrible, and the nausea that came with it was equally bad. She ended up having to have some pain meds after all and having to stay in the hospital for three more days. Her family visited often. Amanda and Robbie visited once, then had to catch their flight home.

Finally, she was allowed to go home, and her entire extended family was there to greet her. There was cake and ice cream, and decorations, and a banner across the front door proclaiming, "Welcome Home Emily!"

It was good to be home. She slept a lot that first month, and then she had to start physical therapy in Clinton. Her therapist was a thin, small-boned, older woman who had a grip like a rock climber. Emily called her the "physical terrorist." She bent her leg and ankle every way possible, and forced Emily to put weight on it and stretch it every day. The physical therapy hurt so much more than the actual break. Emily came out of each session overwhelmed with tears.

She went to therapy three times a week for several months. Gradually, she was able to increase the amount of weight she could put on her leg until she was able to stand on it after a few weeks. A lot of exercises were thrown at her during the sessions, and she was given homework to do later.

Her children would join her in doing the exercises at home, and they made them into games. She had to trace the alphabet with her big toe in the air three times a day, keeping her ankle in place. The children made their toes go round and round twice as fast as she did. Then they did balancing and stretching exercises together. Emily had to balance on her hurt foot while bouncing a ball against a wall. They did that one outside, bouncing balls against the garage door. The children chased after her ball when she missed catching it. Their favorite was sitting on the couch and picking up marbles with their toes and dropping them into a cup. Marbles fell out of their toeholds and rolled everywhere in the living room.

She also did strength training by doing the tractor pull, which was walking out and back in slow steps while pulling against a resistance band. This went on for many months. Recovering became her whole life.

Emily progressed quickly from a wheelchair to a walker, then crutches to a cane, and finally to wearing a special boot until she was able to put her full weight on her leg. She had a plate on her ankle with screws that stuck out, but that would hopefully be removed with time. All her other wounds healed, except her mental ones, because she still had nightmares.

Although she began to be more comfortable with walking and was doing so with less hobbling, her doctor was discouraging.

On one visit, he checked out her leg and remarked, "You are doing well! But I know you want to resume your running career. I don't think it's a good idea for you to do that. It was a bad break, and I would hate to see it break again. You could become a cripple for life."

The thought of never running again was more than she could bear. It was all she wanted any more. When he told her she might have to give it up, she became extremely angry. "I'll show him," she told her husband. "I'll run circles around him one day. I'll run hundreds and hundreds of miles if I want to. He doesn't know everything."

She found a more upbeat sports doctor after that. The new doctor was a woman and an athlete. She told Emily to keep trying and didn't discourage her from running again.

Almost every day, she received an email or a text from Amanda, wishing her well, sending her good vibes, and news about her life. Amanda spent about three months recovering from the race, then started training for the next one. She told Emily all her plans and they discussed her training regimen. Emily encouraged her every time, in spite of her own problems. Emily sent her pictures of her kids, and pictures of her leg during various stages of recovery. The one of her taking her first unaided steps with a victorious smile on her face was the best one.

Emily's children were anxious to help, and did all the household chores without complaint. Her eldest son, Michael, did a lot of the cooking with Emily's help. She had been home schooling them before the accident, and she continued trying to do that during the recovery, but it was just too much. They went off to regular public school, which broke her heart, but they seemed to like it for the most part. Every day they got rides from some family member or friend, as everyone wanted to help. Someone was always available to take Emily to physical therapy, because she had injured her right leg, so for a long time she was unable to drive.

From one day to the next, it was hard to see how things were changing. But she kept a log of her progress and could see changes from week to week, and big ones from month to month. This kept her encouraged and continuously working hard on her recovery.

It was a whole year of torture after the race, and she thought it would never end. Her dreams changed from the attack by the Bad Thing to dreams of herself running again. But once in a while, the Bad Thing swooped down and knocked her off her feet.

While she could imagine running again, she could not imagine running in the world's hardest race ever again. That was too big, too hard, and she was "too soft," but maybe not forever.

Chapter 28: Dreams of Things Yet to Come

Emily wasn't terribly surprised when she got the text from Amanda that she had made it into the race again. The text included several happy, smiley-face symbols and said:

"I'm in, I'm in, I'm in!"

Emily had a feeling that laz, that old softy, would let Amanda enter the race again after the way things had turned out at their last race. He really did want to see a woman finish the race, and Amanda had a lot of potential and drive.

Amanda had become Emily's friend, sending her constant attention and encouragement every day. She seemed to have truly changed from a selfish, jealous woman into a caring, loving person.

While Amanda had plans for being the first woman to ever finish, Emily began to develop plans of her own for far into the future. She wanted to be the second woman to finish, and do it faster than Amanda.

ATTEMPT THREE

Chapter 29: Return to the Yellow Gate

"Amanda!" yelled Emily as she practically fell out of her family's van.

"Emily!" screamed Amanda, running from the bathhouse to the campsite.

They embraced happily, while Emily's children exited the van and ran over to play on the big rock. Their two husbands stood together nearby, talking to each other about nothing in particular.

Amanda and Emily moved to the picnic table of their shared campsite and began reminiscing about the last two years' races.

"Remember Bubba and Bud?" asked Emily. "Bud came to visit me in the hospital after you went home. He brought me flowers!"

"Why, that sweet old fart. Who would have thought he had that in him? And after we were so scared of the two of them when we first saw them," said Amanda.

"You just can't tell what is really in a person's heart until you get to know them," said Emily.

"You're good at that. You never gave up on the two

of us being friends, even when I scraped you."

"I knew it was just your competitive spirit. I really admire that about you," said Emily.

"You are something else," said Amanda.

"Heard dat!" said Emily, laughing. "Are you all ready to go tomorrow?"

"I still have to bag up my food and see the map."

"And eat some chicken!"

"Yeah, and find Ed and give him some more bacon!"

"Oh, I made him some special cookies, too," said Emily.

"He'll be happy. Do you think you're up to hiking up the trail to the Observation Tower tomorrow to see me come up Rat Jaw?"

"I am! I haven't done anything that strenuous yet, but I know I can do it. My kids are all psyched about all of us going up there to cheer you on!"

Michael came running up to give Amanda a hug. The other three children also came over for their share of hugging. Amanda was pleased. She had spent some time with them the previous year before she flew home. She was glad they remembered her and liked her, rather than being mad at her for leaving their mom on Loop Four.

They set up camp and found Ed to give him his gifts. Then they all went up to the Yellow Gate, to check in, get their race bibs, and eat chicken.

Laz thought it was hilarious when he gave Amanda her race bib with the number 1 on it. That meant she was the Human Sacrifice this year, meaning that he thought she would be the one to be left behind for the vultures to eat. But Amanda thought it only meant that she would have to try twice as hard to prove him wrong.

ATTEMPT THREE

Chapter 30: Tour de Force

The race started early the next morning, with Amanda out in the lead. She was the first one around the Yellow Gate, and the first one to turn up the first mountain's trail. Emily's kids were screaming her name for ten more minutes, hoping she would hear them all the way to the top.

Amanda felt more confident this year than she ever had. She made it to the top of the fourteen switchbacks in first place, and flew down the trail along the rocky outcroppings. When she arrived at the Pillars of Death, a bridge of tall eroded rocks with spaces between them, her feet barely touched their tops as she ran across. She tore through the Deep Woods to the coal bench, and then two other racers helped her lift up the massive rock to unearth the book beneath. They gave the book to her first to get her page.

"Here, you got here first," said Jack.

A clot of other competitors were waiting, breathing hard, hoping to get their hands on the book next.

She ripped and ran, stuffing it in her plastic bag and into her pocket as she began descending Jaquemate

Hill. Jack and Rusty stayed right with her, and the three of them navigated to the corner of the park with few problems. They climbed up the trail to the ridge and then down steeply to the confluence and Book 2's hiding spot. By now, she knew exactly where it was.

The climb up Hillpocalypse was always a challenge. She raced on to Book 3, then down into Son of a Bitch Ditch, hauling herself up the other side by grasping the tree root. She checked her bearing through the coal ponds, then hurried up the switchbacks to Book 4 at the Memorial Cairn. The three of them quickly picked up rocks to place on it. For a moment, her mind loosened its tight focus on the race as she remembered the bones of the Bad Thing from last year. She noticed they were still there, and she shuddered.

On they went to the short hill down to the water drop, which was extremely slick this year from all the rain that had drenched the earth in the previous few weeks.

She let Rusty lead through the dense laurel maze of the next area. Finding the pointless new climb and the book in that mess made no sense at all and caused them some grief. They spilled down the Butt Slide, grabbed the page, and then hauled themselves back up the tumble of rocks. They went up through

Bobcat Rock, then up to the Pool and Spa to admire the view from the pond.

On they climbed to Stu's Borehole, then down through the horrible jungle of clawing briers and laurel to get to the highway. They ran out to Middle Finger Ridge to find the dead tree and the book hidden there.

The three of them climbed up the next mountain, crossed the jeep road, and then hiked down to beautiful RawDog Falls. Up they went over Danger Dave's Climbing Wall, then crossed the highway and worked their way up steep Pighead Creek.

Finally, she made it to Rat Jaw and pulled herself up the steep powerline cut by grabbing the old cable off the ground and using her arms to help climb part way to the top. She was breathing hard and her arms and quads were burning when she got close to the road.

A crowd of well-wishers was waiting. Everyone was clapping and yelling. The children were screaming, "Amanda! Amanda!" Emily, Rick, and Robbie were cheering too.

She hiked up the embankment to the jeep road, smiling broadly. They all wanted to hug her, but she couldn't let them as that would be perceived as receiving aid.

She said, "Love you all!" Then she marched up the short hill to the picnic tables next to the Observation Tower to top off all her water levels from the gallon water jugs left there by the park employees. She worked feverishly to drink, eat, and fill up.

Jack and Rusty were right behind her, and they hurried through the ritual of the water drop. She took off first, but they were close behind. Then they were plummeting down Rat Jaw, fearlessly leaping over and through the sharp prongs of the underbrush.

She splashed through the calf-deep water in the storm drain under the prison, vividly remembering Emily's fears from two years before. The frightening aura still hung over the place.

She power-hiked up the Bad Thing, so steep she thought she would run out of air before she got to the top. Rusty and Jack were right on her heels. They didn't have much time or breath for talking. At the Eye of the Needle they took a quick break at the book and ate whatever they had in their front pockets.

Rusty took off first, and Amanda and Jack tore after him, down the steep hill and through the boulder field that was the Zipline. She took a tumble, but rolled right back up on her feet. Only a few cuts and bruises, so she kept going.

Rusty got a little bit turned around before reaching the next book, but Amanda nailed it. She got her page first, then began pushing herself up through Big Hell's steep, open woods.

The capstone area on the top no longer baffled her, and she wove through it to the other side and began the knee-jarring descent on the trail to the main road. She had almost made the first loop.

She breezed over the candyass trail all the way down to camp. Her family and friends had returned from the hike up to the Observation Tower, and they took over provisioning her with food and water. She changed her socks and shoes, and she ate as much as she could. Then she grabbed up her things again, not intending to take a nap. Emily and her children gathered around her to hug her and wish her good luck.

Her Loop One time was amazing. She was the first person back to camp, and in record time. Jack had decided to call it quits, but Rusty was ready to go when she was. They met at the Yellow Gate to travel counterclockwise for the night loop.

All the way back up the trail to the capstones, they met other runners racing in, and everyone was high fiving her and Rusty, yelling, "Good luck! Way to go!"

The remainder of the loop was a blur. They kept up the pace, only stopping twice to eat something, and to get water at the drops. This time Robbie, Emily, and her family were not at the top of Rat Jaw, but she hadn't expected them to hike up in the dark. Two poor, cold souls were there, huddled at the top under a blanket. They shed the blanket and scrambled up to cheer them on.

Amanda got turned around in the laurel maze on the next mountain, but figured it out quickly. That place was always tricky.

They made their way through all the obstacles and returned to camp, where Amanda felt suddenly exhausted. But there was no time for resting yet. Robbie and Rick got Amanda fixed up and turned around, ready to return to the race in twenty minutes.

Rusty met her at the gate again, and off they went on Loop Three, this time travelling the more familiar clockwise direction. They were a team now, bonded by pain.

Loop Three passed in a sleep-deprived haze. She needed sleep desperately by the time they returned to camp. They had completed a Fun Run, but they wanted more. She told Robbie to wake her in one hour and zonked out. One hour went by like a raging torrent of mud. She fought her way out of the mud, then she was out on Loop Four with Rusty again.

This time it was counterclockwise, her least favorite. They attacked the trail up to the capstones, energized by their brief sleep in camp. The descent to the river's fork felt flawless, but they ended up downstream of the book. They quickly realized their mistake and made their way back up to the book.

Climbing up Zipline and then down the Bad Thing felt like a jerky roller coaster ride. Rusty led most of the way, and she had to fight to keep up. At one point, she miserably told him to go on and leave her. But he didn't. She didn't know why. Maybe because it was nighttime and he didn't want to face it alone.

She struggled up Rat Jaw to the Tower, following Rusty's light to stay on track. No one was out to greet them on this loop. She dreamed longingly of being back in camp tucked into her warm sleeping bag.

She caught Rusty as they made their way into the deep laurel mazes of the next mountain, and followed him through the tricky intersections.

They filled up their water containers at the water drop, but had to keep moving because the cold wind was funneling through the gap.

They collapsed near the Memorial Cairn, and both agreed to pass out for a while. She set the timer on her cheap wrist watch, hoping that it worked. In twenty minutes, it went off, and she poked Rusty in the side. They painfully stood up and moved on down to the coal ponds. They slid down the little hill to the boundary trail and jogged along it until it was time to turn off to the knob.

They were starting to get anxious about their time, worrying they might not get into camp with a buffer of time to take another nap. The sleep deprivation was hitting them full on now. Sometimes she wasn't sure which way to go, or even who she was with, but she was very glad to be with someone on this night-time loop.

She had visions of the Bad Thing swooping after them as they went up Jaquemate Hill, remembering Emily's story of the attack the year before. She shook it off, still half unbelieving that it had been anything more than an owl.

When they arrived in camp, bedraggled and foot-sore, they thought of nothing but sleep. If not for the positive energy of their handlers, they would have quit right then. They both took hot showers, but weren't allowed to linger in the warmth. Their crews hustled them through food, drink, and foot aid, then let them collapse for one hour.

They could have slept forever, but they had a meeting with Loop Five, and their crews weren't about to let them lose their focus on the prize they had worked so hard to gain.

ATTEMPT THREE

Chapter 31: The Dream Finish

Rusty was at the Yellow Gate waiting for her as she staggered to the headquarters' campsite.

"Do you want clockwise?" he asked, assuming she preferred it.

"Yes, but it's up to you."

"You can have it," he said magnanimously, always the gentleman. She was glad he was so nice.

"I'll see you out there somewhere," she said. "Don't get lost."

He laughed and took off down the road. The cowbell clanged ominously as she left the safety of the Yellow Gate one final time.

She tried to shake off sleep as she power-hiked up the first mountain. The sleep deprivation was really bad now, although she had managed to get in one hour of sleeping in camp. She ate her scrambled eggs and pickles off a paper plate on the way to the top. Then she hurried. It was going to be a long day.

Her navigation through the remainder of the loop was spot-on most of the time. She got lost in the laurel mazes again, but shook off her confusion and struggled on.

No one was out but her, and the sun was shining. Her mind drifted away on the rays of sunlight, and she lost her focus for brief intervals. At one point, she thought she was running away from the Bad Thing, and she was certain it was coming for her. The fear was real, causing her to pump her legs faster and swivel her neck to see if it was following her.

She was working her way through Bobcat Rock, when suddenly Rusty's head popped through. He looked like a walking zombie, his face pale and his eyes hooded and weary.

Rusty had fallen descending Rat Jaw and cut his knee open. He had bandaged it and wrapped a bandana around it. His arms and legs were all cut up, too. He was grimacing in pain, and favoring his bad leg.

She was glad to see him. They exchanged a few brief words, and then they had to keep moving ever onward in their chosen directions.

There was a crowd at the road up to the Observation Tower this time. Emily was not there, but her eldest son Michael was. He had hiked with the crowd of people up the trail again to see her. Amanda was thrilled to see a friend.

Michael said, "Pretend I'm giving you a high five," and they both hit the air before them.

"Good luck, Amanda!" he shouted as she threw herself down Rat Jaw again.

He had given her a boost of positive energy, and she began to make better time. Before she had met him, she had felt herself to be on a death march. However, the race had become a mental battle, and she quickly lost her drive and resumed the death march as she ascended and descended the next steep peaks.

Her eyelids became heavy and drooping, sometimes closing involuntarily. The next thing she knew, she was on the ground hugging a rock. Had she passed out? She must have been sleep walking. She checked her watch and jumped up in a panic when she realized she had lost fifteen minutes.

She was hungry and nauseous all at the same moment, and she needed to poop. First things first, she remembered Bubba saying. She found a good spot to take care of business. Then she cleaned her hands with the sanitizer she always carried. She found some pre-made almond butter and honey tortillas in her pack, which had smashed up into a gooey ball inside a zip-locked bag. She squeezed the goo into her mouth voraciously, but instantly felt sick and threw it all back up. She started crying, then laughing, in a cycle of mad hysteria, and couldn't stop. She slapped herself hard on the cheek, telling herself this was no time to be losing it.

Everything hurt, especially her feet. She wanted a hot shower and to pick the ticks off her body. Most of all, she wanted her Mom.

Her nose was running and she didn't even care. She didn't bother to wipe it off with her sleeve; she just let it drip like a leaky faucet. She burped and farted simultaneously, and found herself to be truly disgusting. It was ridiculous what she put herself through, all in her quest to reach her goal—the Yellow Gate with laz's face grinning behind it.

Her time was tight as she approached the capstones on the top. She would have to run all out on the trail going down to the park road. She was dead tired, and felt like she was running on fumes. However, the excitement of finishing the race lifted her up and carried her down the mountain. Everything would be worth it if she could just finish the race—all the pain, the suffering, and the years of pushing herself beyond her limits.

"Am I going to make it in time?" she worried incessantly as she descended the mountain.

She ran as fast as her exhausted legs would carry

her all the way to the main road, then up the drive through the campground to where she could see the crowd at the Yellow Gate. The cheering was beyond belief. Laz stood at the Yellow Gate's new pillar, studying his watch.

There was screaming from beyond the Yellow Gate, and people were running down the road towards it. "He's coming! Rusty's coming!"

She saw RawDog standing next to laz at the pillar, and both of them were swiveling their heads back and forth from her to the runner approaching from the other side of the gate. They had enormous smiles on their faces. Laz kept peering at his watch, then looking up to see the finish.

Rusty had the downhill advantage. But she knew he was suffering with his injured knee. She might have a chance.

Rusty made the turn from the bridge, and was in full stride, running like he was in the Olympics 400. She saw Rusty at the same instant that he saw her.

She had about 50 yards left, and she put her legs into overdrive.

"You're not going to beat me!" she screamed into the air, with spit slinging from her mouth.

She just had to win. All the agony of three years of

work to be beaten at the last second? No way could she let that happen. She ran faster.

Time seemed to stop. Her breathing stopped. She flew in mid-air, and her feet stopped touching the ground. She was like a shooting star speeding across the night sky. She would win this day!

She reached out with one hand and touched the Yellow Gate. Rusty's hand slapped the gate right next to hers. Who had won?

"It's Amanda!" yelled laz. "Amanda wins the race by a hair!"

Her husband was right behind her, and he gently turned her wasted body towards him and planted a huge kiss on her lips.

Rusty came around the gate to give her a brief hug.

"59:58!" said laz. "And 22 seconds!"

"Rusty, you had 23 seconds!" he said.

They had just made the 60 hour cut-off. They handed laz their bags of book pages, and he ceremoniously counted them. All pages were accounted for.

She couldn't believe it! She had come in first place, as well as being the first woman to ever finish the race. She was crying and laughing at the same time.

Laz and RawDog were standing at the pillar, beaming like they had a shared secret.

"It was just like our Dream Finish!" said RawDog, excitedly.

"Yeah! Unbelievable!" said laz. "Just like how Coach Carden would have us train in cross country."

Frozen Ed and scRitch stood by them, listening to the two of them talking. A reporter was perched on a rock nearby, furiously writing notes in his notepad. Some media people had a camera trained on laz and RawDog, and were getting footage of their conversation. The group of competitors and visitors crowded around, listening to the story.

"Yeah, we trained hard," mused RawDog, remembering their days of glory. "Coach Carden would take the team out to that one-mile loop road near his house and pit two of us against each other. The two runners would be of pretty similar speeds. We would start at the same time, but racing opposite directions on the loop, then as we rounded the curve to the finish, we would see each other at the same instant and kick it in, giving it all we had. The team members would be watching us, and screaming and cheering. We would touch the tape almost at the same time. It was so exciting," said RawDog.

"Exactly why we put the fifth loop in this race with the final runners racing in opposite directions," nodded laz. "So maybe someday there would be a finish like this. I can't believe it actually happened, after all these years," said laz with satisfaction.

"So, you finally have your Dream Finish," said Kate. She was standing on the embankment above the gate, enjoying the happy celebration.

Laz spoke to Amanda. "You did good! Now I can't say women are too soft ever again!"

The crowd erupted in laughter and applause.

It was the first time to ever finish for both Rusty and herself, and they sat at the gate in chairs of honor, resting, drinking, and eating chicken cooked by scRitch. They answered questions from laz and the media in between bites.

She had never had her picture taken so many times in her entire life. She and Rusty had their picture taken together in front of the Yellow Gate, and then they posed with laz and RawDog. Then Emily and Amanda had their picture taken together. Their families wanted to be in the pictures, too, so they took some more of all of them together.

Laz presented the race cup to both Amanda and Rusty together, in a ceremony with everyone gathered around. The media captured the moment. Laz told them that both their names needed to be engraved on plaques below the cup with their year and finish times. They would each get to have it for six months of the next year, then return it to him for the next year's race.

Finally, Amanda hobbled down to the bathhouse, with Robbie holding her up. The children were skipping ahead of them, and Emily and Rick were following behind.

What a glorious day! She had made history this day, and she was proud. She couldn't stop telling herself, "I did it! I really did it!" It was like a dream, but she was not asleep. Her heart was so full of joy that she thought it might burst like a giant soap bubble.

There were so many things to take care of. She needed a long, hot shower. Her feet needed attention, she needed sleep desperately, and she needed to eat and drink more. But all of that would happen. Right now, she enjoyed the moment of her victory over the mountains, over herself, and over other competitors. It had taken her whole, entire self to finish the race. Despite being wracked with mind-boggling pain and exhaustion, she was exultant.

But there were others to thank. She couldn't have done it without all the aid and encouragement from Robbie, her extended family, and Emily, Rick, and the children. She was humbled by all the help they had given her, and still they were attending to her every need like she was a superstar. She said, "Thank you!" a million times. She hugged Emily and said, "This one was for you, Em!"

Chapter 32: The White Gate

Amanda and Robbie spent the following week at Emily's house in nearby Briceville. It was vacation time for them, and Amanda wanted to recover some from the race and spend time with Emily. The family moved the boys into the den so Amanda and Robbie could have their bedroom.

Emily pampered Amanda the whole week with scrumptious cooking and plenty of attention. Robbie spent time walking the property and playing with the kids. Rick had to go to work, but he spent the evenings hosting them.

At the end of the week, Amanda was walking better, and felt like getting out of the house. Emily suggested they all visit the park and take some more pictures with the Yellow Gate. That sounded like fun to Amanda, so they all piled into the family van and drove the winding road to the park.

They drove to the trailhead sign and parked, planning to walk from there. The kids ran down to the big rock to pretend to be mountain climbers, and Robbie went with them to supervise. Amanda and Emily walked slowly up to the headquarters' campsite. It was strange to be in the park when the race was not being held. A lot of the campsites were empty, but the headquarters' campsite was in use.

The stacked rock pillars for the gate were there, but the Yellow Gate itself was missing. "Where is it?" asked Amanda, looking about.

She saw it up ahead right before the bridge over the creek; it was lying flat on sawhorses. Two park employees were there, bent over and working hard. They had sanded down the old gate, removing all the ancient, chipped yellow paint and rust. Now they were painting it a pure, lustrous, clean white.

The Yellow Gate was no more. Now it would forever be known as the White Gate.

Emily stood there looking at it, shaking her head in puzzlement. "White! Why white?" she asked.

"I don't know," said Amanda, shrugging her shoulders.

But later she thought to herself: *How appropriate!*

It seemed like the perfect canvas for the new age of the world's hardest race now that a woman had broken down the barrier.

Everything changes…

*Translation for Amanda's Entry Essay:
"I will be the first woman to finish this race no matter what. You have my word on that. I am not too soft!"
*Translation for response from laz:
"All women are too soft!"

Made in the USA
Coppell, TX
07 February 2020

15524256R00095